the indigo girls

PENNI RUSSON

ALLEN&UNWIN

Allen & Unwin
83 Alexander St
Crows Nest NSW 2065
Australia
Phone: (61 2) 8425 0100
Fax: (61 2) 9906 2218
Email: info@allenandunwin.com
Web: www.allenandunwin.com

ISBN 978 1 74237 768 1

Design based on cover design by Tabitha King and Kirby Stalgis
Text design by Kirby Stalgis
Set in 12.5/16.5 pt Spectrum MT by Midland Typesetters, Australia
Printed in China at Everbest Printing Co.

10 9 8 7 6 5 4 3 2 1

Chapter One
Zara

I spent the whole long drive to Indigo plugged into my iPod and texting Sooz. Sooz wanted to know what my brother, Ivan, was doing. All my friends have a crush on him, he's kind of good looking, I guess. And he's got this whole doesn't-talk-to-anyone thing going on, which girls seem to find irresistible. I try and tell them he's a complete dork but they never listen. Like in the car, Ivan had his PDA out, flicking around the little pen thing that you use to write on the screen. 'Cause you need an organiser when you go camping. As if. Why can't he just have a PSP like a normal person? It bugs me. I didn't answer her texts about Ivan.

Kayla texted me too: *poor baby* — she always calls all of us baby, secretly it annoys me — *two weeks of family torture*. At first

1

I wasn't going to answer her text either. But eventually I punched in a totally non message. It seemed too rude not to say anything. After all, as far as she knew, we were still friends. Then Sooz again: *See you on the flip side.* The flip side? What did that even mean?

Dad was driving. Mum was just kind of staring vacantly out the window. Dad was talking but he wasn't actually talking *to* Mum, or to anyone for that matter, it's just this pointless airfill thing that he does, a running monologue about petrol prices and fishing and car accident hotspots and the dangers of roundabouts. Did I mention that my dad is a cop?

About three years ago, my brother Ivan and I noticed that my parents don't talk anymore. Not to each other. They talk to us, of course, and sort of through us. I don't even know if they realise. But Mum will be in the kitchen and she'll say, 'Could you ask Dad to start the barbeque?' and I'll go into the lounge room and ask him even though Mum could lean across the kitchen bench and call through the open door to ask him herself. He's, like, sitting right there! Or I ask Dad if I can go shopping with Kayla and the other girls and he says, 'Well, I don't know, Zara. Ask your mother. Has she got any plans this afternoon?' And I'm like, but you *live* together. And you don't know if she 'has plans'? I don't say this, though. What's the point?

One day, it was just me and Ivan in the kitchen. He was biting into a sandwich, he totally inhales two loaves of bread a day. I asked him, 'What about when they . . . you know?'

He almost spat out his food. 'Zara! I'm eating here. They *don't*. Do they?'

'Well, they've done it at least once in your lifetime or I wouldn't be here,' I pointed out.

'You're so disgusting.'

I snorted. 'In complete silence, though. That's sort of spooky. Like *Stepford Wives*.'

Ivan leaned on the counter, his shoulders shaking with laughter. 'Or they mutter away to themselves. "Oh my, is that the time . . . now I really must . . ." Or like when they're in the car, "Now, did I mean to go left or right here?" only they'd be saying . . .'

'Don't!' I yelled, alarmed that he would get more graphic. He tried to say more, but he couldn't get it out he was laughing so hard. I covered his mouth with both my hands, whimpering between laughs, 'No! Nooooo.'

Mum walked in. 'What's so funny?' she asked, smiling like she was ready to share the joke but with this almost desperate edge, like the girls at school who aren't popular but want to be.

Suddenly it wasn't funny anymore, for either of us. The last laugh wheezed out and Ivan took his sandwich into the lounge room to eat it. I picked up my mobile, flicking through the address book like it was suddenly crucial or something, so I didn't have to look at her face. Do they even love each other? I mean, are all old people joyless like them? Or is it just my parents? Tilly's parents aren't joyless. They really like each other, you can just tell. I bet they talk all the time, about books and movies and stuff. And about Tilly and Teddy of course. Do Mum and Dad talk about me and Ivan?

So anyway, we arrived at Indigo and found our spot near the toilets and the kiosk and we all got out and Dad winched up the caravan, and Mum started setting out the stove and the cups to make tea because that's what they always do. This is, like, their life. And Ivan stayed in the car with his PDA and I looked around for Mieke and Tilly but I couldn't see them. So I leaned against the car, looking bored. It's an art to look that bored. Botox-bored, Sooz calls it. People spend thousands on plastic surgery to look like I did right then.

Mum made tea and these sort of spongy, flabby tomato-and-cheese sandwiches.

Finally Tilly rocked up, waving like crazy out the window of her car and I dropped the bored expression and flipped up a wave.

That was when I got the text message. I almost didn't read it because I thought it was Kayla again, and Kayla was a million miles away, back in Melbourne. But it wasn't Kayla, anyway. It was Mieke — to both Tilly and me.

Just found out yesterday that I got a late place in Drew Svenson's summer class. He's an awesome painter. Happy face but sad face. Not coming to Indigo for another whole week! Oh no. Mieke xx

I read the text through twice. I don't know why, but I felt this heavy pit in my stomach. Part of Indigo, a huge part, was Mieke. Without her it would be . . . different.

4

I wasn't interested in different. I mean, I was happy for her and stuff, if this painter was so great. But why did she have to go to school in the holidays? It had never been just me and Tilly before. I mean, Tilly's nothing like me. What if it wrecked everything?

I was about to turn my phone off when another message came through. I had my finger on the off button – I nearly ignored it. I should have, because it was another one of *those* messages, the kind I've been getting lately – from 'number withheld'.

This one said: *You are a pricktease.*

'Everything all right?' Mum asked.

'The batteries are running low.' I deleted the message and switched the phone off. When I looked up, Ivan was watching me. The freak. I gave him a look, then stared at my nails. Bored. Bored. Botox-bored.

•

Chapter Two
Tilly

Summer always seems to start when we get to Indigo. Christmas and December, it's like summer's dress rehearsal. It isn't really summer until we turn down the dirt road, until we see Point Indigo for the first time, until we see the blue sparkling ocean.

Every summer since I was nine years old and my baby sister Teddy was four, we've camped at Indigo foreshore. Teddy and Tilly. Because what my parents really wanted was a pair of golden retrievers. Actually, we're Matilda and Theodora but the only people who call us that are a few stray great-aunts. And Mum when she's livid. And relief teachers who don't know any better.

Dad and I started putting up the tent pretty much as

soon as we leapt out of the car. Mum and Teddy disappeared because Dad and I have firm ideas about tent erection and if they hang about, it all ends in tears. Mum's usually, then Teddy's. It's all about birth order. Dad and I are both firstborns, right? So we organise and we're the boss. Which sometimes means we clash because we both want to be the boss of each other, but usually it works out pretty well when we're both the boss of something else, like the tent, or Teddy.

Anyway, while I was helping Dad I was thinking about Mieke's text message. I was trying not to think of it as a disaster but frankly, I found the whole thing a little unsettling.

You see, it's such a fine balance, the whole Indigo Girl thing. Zara's an alpha, right? Which is the first letter of the Greek alphabet and also another way of saying she's a dominant chick. She's popular. In fact, according to this girl I know, Jess, who used to go to Zara's school, Zara is *the* most popular girl at her school, hands down.

Zara's *amazing* to look at. Golden-haired, golden-skinned. Princess Zara. She doesn't see it like that. She calls herself a meat-and-potatoes girl because she's blonde and tall and easy on the eye, which most guys are into. She says she's just a combination of unchallenging factors — the hair, the blue eyes, the C cup. According to Chris Timms in my Year 8 metalwork class, 'More than a handful's a waste.' He meant me, I guess. Not that he would know, mind you, it's not like he — or anyone else — has tried (is that a smidge of regret in my voice? Not about Chris Timms . . .

but if it was someone else, a particular someone, I might not completely disapprove of the experiment). Anyway, back to Zara's factors: eyes, hair, boobs, tall, thin . . . 'Yada yada yada,' Zara would say, and she'd look bored while she was saying it. This, mind you, is when Mieke and I would throw clumps of damp, smelly seaweed at her, because she's actually really and truly beautiful.

Now me, I'm not an alpha obviously. I'm not, like, omega or anything which is the *last* letter in the Greek alphabet and saved for people like Finlay Ridge who's got this really unfortunate forehead and spits when he talks and reads books about assembling machine guns. I'm more like one of the obscure ones in the middle that no one's ever heard of – omicron or something. Gingery, freckly, a bit pointy in the face – nose, chin, even my cheekbones look sort of excruciating. Sometimes I *feel* sharp. All over, even on the inside, as if there's something unapproachable about me, something spiky and ouchy, though most of the time I'm harmless.

And Mieke, well, she's sophisticated . . . maybe a delta. Fourth from the top, kind of aloof. If aloof was a shape it would probably be a triangle and the Greek letter delta is a triangle. Mieke's cool in an arty, slightly gothic way. Her mum's a fashion designer. Her dad's a graphic illustrator and does these really dark, postmodern, brooding comics. The whole family is steeped in arty coolness. And Mieke is carrying the family torch, only it's more like a family candelabrum, one of those really ornate ones.

Mieke's beautiful too, or I think she is, but in a different way from Zara. You know there are some flowers that look small and delicate, but then when you go to pick them the stems nearly rip your hand in half because they're so resilient and wiry? That's Mieke. Small, but not cute. *She* thinks she's looked nine years old for the past seven years. She says when she hears her voice played back, like on a phone message, she sounds like a kindergarten boy with a lisp (she doesn't have a lisp). And she says she looks like she's always got two black eyes. She's kind of pale.

If Mieke and Zara and I all went to the same school there's no way we'd be friends. It doesn't take a rocket scientist to work that out. Alphas and deltas and omicrons, they just don't belong together in the real world.

Especially alphas and omicrons. This is where the fine balance comes in. Mieke, as a delta, is a buffer, a halfway point, a mediator. She knows what it's like to be cool, so she and Zara share a common language even though Zara is cool in a totally different way. But Mieke also respects the pointy brain. So we've got our own thing going on. And somehow it makes me and Zara work too.

I was thinking about this stuff when Zara came over. I stood up and brushed dirt off my hands, suddenly shy. I started off every summer feeling a bit shy, like a part of me worried that this was the summer Zara and Mieke would turn around and say, 'Who do you think you are, Matilda Katherine Dove?' And who *do* I think I am? No one much, not compared to this girl. She leaned down and air kissed each cheek, as if she were an elegant relative at a funeral and I was a slightly pudgy, stumpy child.

'It's so good to see you,' Zara said. 'Can you believe Mieke's not coming?'

'I know. It will be fully weird without her. Like the two musketeers.' As soon as I said it, I regretted it. Was it presumptive of me to call us the two anything?

But Zara sailed on smoothly. 'Yeah, totally.'

'Omigosh, like Zara! It's like, so totally rad to see you.' That was my dad. He's always making fun of how my friends and I talk.

'Dad! No one says *rad*. That's so 80s.'

'Hi, Mr Dove,' Zara said. She's really polite around parents.

'Call me Julian. Mr Dove sounds so wet.'

'And yet Julian is so manly,' I said.

'That's right,' said Dad. And he went back to the tent, obviously pleased that I was talking to Zara so he could be the boss of it all by himself.

'Where's Teddy?' Zara asked. For some reason Zara adores Teddy. I mean Teddy is adorable (ninety-nine per cent of the time) but Zara doesn't seem the type to like little kids.

'She's around somewhere.' This was my chance. I tried to sound nonchalant. 'Where's Ivan?' I felt momentarily sick, because what if he hadn't come this year?

Zara rolled her eyes. 'I don't know. Sitting in the car or something. He's such a social reject. Like he's twenty, and he's still coming on this lame family camping trip. What's with that?'

I wanted to defend him. But he's a boy-Zara. An alpha. A golden boy. I would die if Zara knew how I felt about him and I would die a million times more if Ivan knew. Besides, I know it really annoys Zara when her friends have crushes on him. And he obviously doesn't give her friends a second thought, because he's three years older than us, which means he's already done two whole years of university and we're only going into Year 12 next year.

Year 12. Sigh. I'm so ready for uni. High school is boring. I have this vision that university is going to be full of other people like me, pointy brain people, and we'll sit around and talk about literature (you know, for fun) and the homoerotic subtext in *Star Trek* (which is one of my favourite things to do 'cause as soon as you decide to make everyone on *Star Trek* secretly gay it gets heaps funnier) and everything will have this learned glow about it, like you can suck up knowledge just walking down the halls.

Anyway, I wanted to defend Ivan and I also wanted to say that family camping trips aren't lame and that I'll probably still be coming when I'm twenty, but then I worried that she would think *I* was lame. So I just nodded, apologising to Ivan in my brain, which was probably the closest I would get to talking to him all summer.

'Are you sleeping in the annexe this year?' I asked Zara. She hated the stuffy annexe. But she hated being inside the caravan with her parents more.

'Nuh-uh,' she said, with a grin. 'Guess what I scored for Christmas?'

We walked up the dirt road to her campsite and she pulled a canvas bag out from the floor of her car. She rolled it out. It was one of those tiny one-person tents that's almost really a sleeping bag, sausage shaped around the legs but opening out around the head.

'My own swag,' she said, proudly.

'Ugh,' I shuddered.

'What?'

'It's so small! It looks like a coffin.'

'No way. I love it. Just me, no one to bug me. Out under the stars.'

See, I don't get that. Our family tent has three rooms — a sitting-type room, Mum and Dad's bedroom, and Teddy and I share the other room. I like having Teddy there. I like that there's only a thin canvas separating me and Mum and Dad so I can hear them breathe and snore and turn over in their sleep. Zara would think that was weird. Maybe I am weird. But won't she be scared, all on her own in the middle of the night? Won't she be lonely? Or is that just part of being Zara, sleeping out under the stars on her own?

'I better go back and help Dad,' I said.

'Yeah, I'll put this up.'

That was something I liked about Zara. She wasn't precious. She wasn't afraid to get dirty or break a nail. She did stuff for herself.

'I'll see you at the rockpool after dinner?'

We always met there on the first night. It was tradition.

'Yep.'

I walked back up to our campsite, which is at the quiet end. Mum and Dad like having lots of trees around us. Zara's mum likes being close to the facilities.

I was still thinking about Zara. You know what my mum's going to say? She's going to say that the up side of Mieke not coming till later is that it will give me and Zara a chance to get to know each other better. But is that a good thing? What if we get to know each other and she realises just how many Greek letters there are between alpha and omicron? What if this *is* the summer she finally says she doesn't want to hang out with me anymore?

'What if it is?' says inner-Mum.

'I don't think I could handle that kind of rejection,' I answer out loud. 'Besides, I like being an Indigo Girl. It's fun. And it's kind of special. Like a holiday from me.' Inner-Mum nods knowingly and takes a memo for later. *Wants to take a holiday from self.*

Mum (my real mum, that is, not inner-Mum which is, let's be honest, just me talking to myself) is a psychotherapist, which doesn't mean she's a therapist who's psycho, because that's one of those jokes that gets old fast. She's like a cross between a psychiatrist and a counsellor. She's a trained doctor (like a psychiatrist) but she believes in something called cognitive behavioural therapy instead of prescribing drugs, which means she tries to make you change the way you think. Anyway, I'm sure having a mum who's a psychotherapist messes with your head because there I was, walking along talking to myself.

And there was Ivan, watching me talking to myself. 'Who's the social reject now?' I muttered.

'Pardon?' he said.

'What?' I said. I know, this is classic material. So worth recording for posterity.

'Were you talking to me?'

'Oh. Um. No,' I said. Monosyllabic much?

He looked around. 'You do realise there's no one else here?'

'I know.' You know there are those girls who can blush a pretty rose colour and boys are apparently enchanted by it and therefore you get away with being a complete idiot? Yeah, well, I can't do that.

Though, bless him, he looked more confused than scornful.

I explained. 'I was talking to myself. You know. As you do.'

'As you do,' he said, quite kindly really. His eyes even crinkled a bit like he was thinking about smiling sometime this millennium.

I walked away grinning maniacally to myself because you know what? I might have been sprung talking to myself, but in other news, Ivan Sutherland and Tilly Dove just had a conversation.

That night we cooked vegies on the barbeque: potato sliced thin, sprinkled with salt, pepper and rosemary, plus eggplant, zucchini, tomato and asparagus. We argued about whether or not to put salt on the asparagus. I did when Dad wasn't looking.

Zara's dad, Tony, came over and cooked their sausages on the hot plate next to ours. The dads all bonded over us when we were younger and they had to keep an eye on us. They hung out together on the beach while we played. But they don't actually have much in common. Zara's dad is a cop. Mine teaches political science at uni. Not completely unrelated, I guess. Still, maybe it's just me, but conversation doesn't exactly flow.

We were all standing around cooking, Tony doing his sausages, and me and Dad with our stuff — we both like to be the boss of the barbeque too and we were arguing over possession of the spatula due to a difference in technique (much flipping back and forth versus wait, then flip *once*, then wait) — when along came Ivan.

'Hey, Dad,' he mumbled. 'Mum wants to know if you want red wine or white tonight.' Then Ivan turned to my dad and said, 'Hi, Professor Dove.'

'Call me Julian, please,' Dad said waving a barbeque fork around, generally in my direction because I'd won possession of the spatula. He should watch it or Tony will arrest him for being armed and dangerous. Then Dad said to me, 'Ivan was in my Language and Law class last year.'

I looked at Dad. He was? I sent little telepathic dagger points into Dad's brain. How could something like that get by me?

'It was a great class.' Ivan was looking at me when he said that, so I nodded. Smooth.

'Are you going on with Political Science this year?' Dad asked Ivan.

'It's my major.'

'What subjects are you doing?' I asked. It was as if I was two people inhabiting the one body. As long as I was talking to Dad or Tony I was fine, but anything I said to Ivan made me sound like I was twelve years old. Talking underwater. In a second language.

'Love, Family and Sexuality,' Ivan answered. 'World Politics in Transition. Australia in Conflict. And Transforming Terrorism.'

How cool are those subjects?

'Love, Family and Sexuality is one of mine,' said Dad. 'And you'll probably have Nina Rosse for Australia in Conflict. I think you'll like her.'

'*You* teach a subject about love and sexuality?' I said to Dad. 'Eew!'

Ivan looked at me seriously. 'It's about the interaction between public and private realms in terms of legislation and legal practice.'

Well, der. How stupid does he think I am?

'Actually it's all about you and your sister,' Dad said, winking. 'I start every year with a slideshow of baby photos.'

'It's amazing they let you teach it at all,' I retorted, 'considering you couldn't get a date till you were twenty-five. And then you married the first woman who was desperate enough to go out with you.'

Tony was turning over the sausages with this weird half smile on his face and Ivan was staring at me, looking a bit shocked. Dad's students always take him really seriously, 'cause he's a professor. I reckon he only became a professor because Dr Dove sounded so stupid. Anyway, I don't think the Sutherlands muck around like this with each other.

'Sparkling,' Tony said to Ivan. 'There's a bottle in the esky. Tell your mother the sausages will be ready in five minutes.'

If the sausages are going to be ready in five minutes, you'd think Tony could tell her himself and then Ivan could stay here and talk to me. But Tony was as immune to my telepathic daggers as Dad, and Ivan left, looking longingly behind him. Not at me, though: at our vegetables. Because they smelled, if I do say so myself, pretty damn good. Who'd want to eat nasty suburban mystery bags — lips and bums, Teddy would say — when you can eat friendly organic vegies like these? No animals were harmed in the making of our meal.

Dad and Tony started talking about football. Yawn. With a longing look of my own at the vegies, I left them to the mercy of Dad and went to find Teddy and Mum to oversee the making of the couscous, which we'd left in their incapable hands.

Chapter Three
Zara

I was waiting for Tilly, sitting on the sand, wearing my headphones but my iPod wasn't switched on. I was looking out at the sea. Sometimes you look at the sea and it's this amazing powerful force of nature and sometimes it's just big and blank and empty. It was a blank empty day. There was still an hour or so until the sun set, but the light was already changing into this intensely yellow colour, so everything shone extra bright. Ivan once told me it was the infra-red that made that happen. I don't know about stuff like that, but I love the light like this, long and yellow.

I wasn't actually bored, but I could tell I was making the face. Sometimes it creeps up on me, maybe because I've done it too many times. Like when you were a little kid and your mum said, 'If you keep making that face the wind will change and you'll be stuck with it.' Which is a totally crappy thing to say. I mean, how freaky! I'm never going to be a mother. But maybe my mother was right and the wind had changed and I was just going to look bored forever.

I couldn't get 'number withheld' out of my head. Was it Marcus sending them? Would he really do that? Part of me was sure he wouldn't, not after all the time we spent together. But if it wasn't him, who would it be? It *had* to be Marcus. I knew he was angry with me. But if anyone should be angry it was me, right? I didn't feel angry, though. Looking out to sea, I felt nothing. I felt blank, empty.

Tilly arrived. She sat next to me on the sand. I smiled at her, it was good to see her.

'I keep expecting Mieke to show up,' I said.

'I know. It's *surreal* without her here.'

Tilly always uses words like that. She's really smart. Not like Ivan, who's just completely nerdy, plugged into his computer most of the time. She's smart in an ordinary everyday kind of way, like when we go to the Indigo cinema she always notices extra things about the story and the characters, symbolism and stuff.

'I even miss their caravan,' I said. It's a corrugated tin A-frame that Mieke's parents made themselves.

'Me too. It's a real Indigo icon.'

After we'd talked about Mieke we were silent for a minute.

'So how was your year?' I asked Tilly. We don't really stay in touch away from Indigo. We don't email or SMS or anything. And Tilly and I even live on the same trainline. Though it's a long trainline. I'm out in the 'burbs, where it's all cul-de-sacs and families and enormous houses with three lounge rooms and stuff. Tilly's sort of on the fringe of the city, lots of groovy little terrace houses and cafes and bars and cinemas and designer clothes. My school's massive and it's known for sport and computers and science. You know, just regular subjects. At her school they do philosophy. Plus they have this big sound studio and they do dance for VCE. I know because my best friend from primary school, Jess, moved there after the end of Year 6. Jess and I don't keep in touch either. I tried at first and so did she, but then we just kind of drifted apart.

'It was all right,' said Tilly. 'The usual. You?'

'Fine,' I said.

We asked each other all the same questions we ask every year, speaking the universal language of high school. What subjects did you do, what were your teachers like, all that stuff.

Mostly I looked out at the sea, though sometimes I looked at Tilly while she was speaking. She has a strange face. You could almost think she was ugly, I guess, because she has a really pointy chin and nose. She has heaps of freckles and her hair is a gingery brown colour and sort of frizzy and she always wears it in a ponytail, always. She's far and away the best swimmer of all of us, though on land she moves kind of slow and heavy. She hides her body shape with loose-fitting clothes — big T-shirts and baggy shorts mostly — which is weird because in bathers she's sort of strong looking, solid. Not completely girly, but there's still something cool about her body — like, I remember reading in a magazine once that you don't have to be pretty to be sexy and at the time I didn't get it but looking at Tilly, I realised it's sort of true. Also she has this really amazingly full bottom lip and she always looks like she's wearing lipstick even though I know she's not. And there's something about her face that I like looking at, even though she's not *pretty* pretty, if you know what I mean.

A couple of guys, surfers, were heading out with their boards to use the last of the daylight. I watched them stepping through the waves, calling to each other.

Suddenly I was hanging out for it, the first surf of the summer. I'm not a surfie chick or anything. I don't live to surf, waiting for the next wave. Well, it'd be a pretty pathetic life where we live, a couple of hours drive from the nearest surf beach, and I don't even have a car. It's not like Mum and Dad would take me to the beach just to go surfing.

But a couple of years ago Tilly, Mieke and I went to surf school here in Indigo, which was, like . . . I can't tell you how much fun it was. It's one of the only times in my life I remember being completely carefree. At first we were all really bad at it. But then Tilly knelt up and caught a wave and we were all really excited for her. And then I got to my feet and stayed standing for a whole minute. It wasn't a competition. It was *funny* and crazy and exciting, getting this skill together, making it happen. We kept bobbing up out of the water, being hit in the face with our surfboards and laughing at ourselves and each other. After that I got a surfboard for my birthday and I was so looking forward to more surf school but Chris, the local guy who taught it, was gone, moved up to the city. We still go surfing every year, Tilly, Mieke and me. Sometimes we see Chris out there, back in town, visiting his folks, surfing home waters, always happy to give us some tips, shouting encouragement to tackle the big waves. There's even surf lifesaving a few times a year at school. But somehow it's never felt quite the same as it did that summer, when none of us were good at it and nobody cared.

When I got back up to camp, Dad was getting the Land Cruiser ready to take the waveskis, paddles and surfboards down to the beach box. There's a row of them down on the beach — old fashioned bathing boxes. Mum reckons they cost the earth, like enough to house a whole family, but Dad bought one anyway a couple of years ago and even Mum's glad he did because now she's got somewhere shady to sit and we can store our table and chairs and umbrellas. For Mum it's almost like she's not really at the beach at all.

'Want to come, Zars?' Dad asked. 'I could use a hand.'

I shrugged. 'Sure.'

Me and Dad don't say a lot to each other. Actually Dad doesn't talk to anyone much, just sort of at the world. Sometimes I think maybe he and I are alike, though everyone always says I'm just like Mum was when she was my age. I know that makes Mum really proud, like we've got this special connection, but I *hate* it when people say that.

I used to really worship Dad. When you're in kindergarten, having a dad who's a policeman is the coolest thing. Well, except maybe if he was a fireman. He'd come to school every year in his uniform to talk to my class about road safety or stranger danger or whatever, and at first I'd be all like, 'That's *my* dad.' And then later I just sort of didn't say anything, and then when I was in about Year 5 I begged him not to come. I remember the look on his face when Mum chimed in with, 'She's right, Tony, it would be complete social suicide. It wasn't so bad when she was younger but she's practically a teenager now.' Like we'd slapped him.

But then he just looked normal again. He nodded once and walked out of the room. Mum smiled at me, one of her big fake 'I'm on *your* side' mother–daughter, go team smiles. I'd walked out too, disgusted with her, disgusted with myself. But still relieved that Dad wasn't coming to my school, convincing myself that Dad didn't care, knowing how much he really did.

It's almost like I can pinpoint it to that very day that I stopped being 'Daddy's girl'. Like he decided that I was my mother's daughter and everyone else sort of agreed, and that was that.

We were heading up the track that wound back out of the campground so we could take the road to the main carpark where the beach boxes were. It was that grainy time of day, the light was going. He turned into the main road.

'Dad, look out!'

The Land Cruiser stopped with a jolt, veering left. A huge roo stared into the headlights, then put its front paws down and continued crossing with a lazy hop, like of course we should stop for it.

'Are you all right?' Dad asked me.

'I'm fine.' My nails were digging into my palms. He clutched the steering wheel for a minute, staring at the deserted road. Then he eased into reverse, straightened the car and kept driving.

That night I lay in my one-person tent. Tilly was wrong. It wasn't a coffin. It was a cocoon. Beyond the mesh of the mosquito net I could see stars. It was warm, the air clear in my lungs, filled with the smell of eucalyptus and the sea. It was good to be away from the city, from the cars that whined up and down all night on the freeway near our house.

Like I did every night, I thought about what it would be like to drive across the country when I finished school, just me and this swag. I'd camp by the side of the road, heading north when winter hit the south, following the sun.

It's been my thing for a year or two now, my plan, but I'd always imagined someone going with me. For a while

24

it was Marcus. We even talked about it, in an offhand kind of way (though for some reason I never mentioned the savings in my bank account: the money I earned slinging lattes at the Loveshack, added to the money my grandma gave me a few years ago). I'd thought about taking Kayla, Sooz, Rio and Tang Yi — though seriously, I doubted they could hack it. Anyway, I wouldn't want to anymore. Not Kayla. And if Kayla didn't go, Sooz wouldn't.

Sometimes last year I even imagined Tilly and Mieke coming with me — it made sense, after all. They were already my camping buddies. Mieke might do it too, but I knew Tilly wouldn't, not just heading off for a year or more. She'd be off to uni as soon as she finished Year 12.

Anyway, that's how I used to see it, me and a gang of girls, or maybe just one boy. But when I got the swag the dream changed. Now in the dream I'm alone. Heading for the Northern Beaches or the Red Centre, window down, wind in my face, on an empty, open road. Just driving, really. Who cares where?

Chapter Four
Tilly

Teddy was asleep beside me in the tent and she was making this funny whinnying sound when she snored, like Big Bird. So I was lying there awake, waiting to adjust to it, thinking about what was wrong with me.

And I think I worked it out. This is what is wrong with me: I'm a weird mutant hybrid. (Warning: long and rambling rant to follow. Stay with me on this.)

So, on the one hand I'm still a kid. I'm awkward and gormless, I know nothing about the world. Nothing practical anyway, nothing useful about life. I mean, I know who the prime minister of Denmark is, right? But on the other hand I'm sort of this mini-adult and have been forever. For instance, next year I'll be eighteen. Which is great, but not for the reasons you think. It's not the right to drink rum and coke legally at a bar or buy cigarettes over the counter. What excites me is that I'll be able to vote. Partly because voting's all about me and what I think, and also because there's this orderly part of my brain that likes filling out forms. But mostly it's because I want to be taken seriously by people in power and voting is a way for that to happen. Plus someone has to vote the good guys in and the seriously bad guys out. Am I right? (Colour me a greener shade of green.)

Anyway, so I *know* that's geeky, but I don't really understand why. I missed something, some important part of my development. I mean ages ago, right back in Year 7. It's as if there's this whole other *The Lion, the Witch and the Wardrobe* world at school and I couldn't find the right wardrobe — everyone else is already up to the bit where the lion gets hacked up on the table and I'm still fumbling about in the coats.

Or it's like a tribe with its own language and native dress and all these sacred rituals and totems and I'm a total outsider. And you know what they say about how you can't observe from outside because as soon as you observe you've changed the conditions — so just by being there you've kind of wrecked it? That's how I feel all the time. As if I'm this really obvious white-coated, black-rimmed-glasses-wearing scientist and the other kids at school just sit there waiting for me to go away so they can get back to being real teenagers.

But it's not just a secret code in words, it's shoes and everything. A language of shoes. But how do I get the code? When did they give that out? Was I sick that day? What *happens* to adults who were never teenagers? What happens to girls like me? Do we become those crusty spinster aunts who have thirteen cats and mutter constantly to ourselves? 'Cause I've already started doing that!

Zara's got it, for sure. She's got the code. Maybe she *is* the code. Maybe the code is a girl, maybe it's all those girls who seem hardwired for popularity — the best dressed, the shiniest, the girls who get the best dressed and shiniest guys. It's not just looks or having the right clothes. It's a sort of electricity. You can tell those girls, you know, even from other schools, you see them in waiting rooms or on the train or at interschool events. And you just know.

I'm not a friendless wonder or anything. I know people. I always have someone at school to hang out with. But they're just other omicrons like me, others that were left stranded on the beach when the tide of popularity went out. They're not . . . it sounds awful saying this, but they're not the people I would *choose* to be my friends. Don't get me wrong, some of them are really nice people. (I can't believe I'm saying this. If they ever found out I would die of shame.) But I can't help feeling as if I've missed out on something. That maybe that world, you know, the one through the wardrobe, is worth seeing. Maybe I *want* to see it, maybe I even want to be queen of it for just one day.

End of rant. I guess I finally got used to Teddy's Big

Bird snores, because I went to sleep and had odd, awkward dreams about wardrobes and alpha girls and being in a play where I was the only one who didn't know the lines.

Breaking into the golf club is an annual tradition with us, harking all the way back to the first summer.

There we were, three nine-year-old girls. Life was different back then. Don't get me wrong, Zara and Mieke were still way cooler than me, but I didn't know it and neither did they. We found each other at the beach, you know, 'cause we were all nine and that's how simple it is when you're nine. Actually Zara found Teddy. Zara played with Teddy first and then with me and Teddy. And then I can't remember how Mieke ended up playing with us, I think her mum and my mum were talking. They still get on really well, Mum and Sumi.

Anyway, nine years old and we wanted to go and look at the golf club up the other end of the beach. It started as a dare. When we played truth or dare, I always picked truth. I didn't really have any secrets, so I had nothing to lose. Zara always picked dare. Actually we stopped playing years ago, but I remember that. She never once picked truth. I think it was Zara's dare but it was so inspired and exciting, it became all our dare.

The golf club was brand new then, and even our parents were in awe of it. Zara's dad and my dad went up to have a look at it and came back coughing and spluttering about how much it cost to play there. Then the mums went to the restaurant one night and had cocktails and came back in the dark giggling their heads off – we could hear them staggering up the dirt track. Mum and Sumi were singing 'Lola' by The Kinks and Zara's mum was pretending to be sober and trying to shush them. I remember Mum collapsing into bed and declaring loudly, 'I'm drunk as a skunk.' Teddy thought she was hilarious and I was self-righteous and cross and lectured her all the next day about the dangers of alcohol while she laughed and moaned and clutched her head.

Zara was the one who decided we should dress up, because it was so fancy. None of us had good clothes (we *were* camping) but we managed to scrape up three skirts between us (Mieke wore a long black one of her mum's that dragged along behind her) and Zara raided her mum's make-up. We also made our own jewellery with shells and stuff. And because we didn't have high heels Zara made us all walk on tiptoe. We must have looked hilarious tottering up the beach. Our mums didn't have the hearts to stop us.

So when I say breaking in, I really just mean we walked in through the front gates. Well, the back gate actually, since we came up the path from the beach. There's the golf club itself, which to us was super boring, it just looked like a restaurant, with a small shop selling ridiculously expensive hats, plus of course the greens in between the dunes. I don't play golf but if I did, I'd want to play it there. It's awesome, startlingly perfect green lawns in between big sandy dunes. And then there's the mini resort: ritzy accommodation where the golfers and the families (mostly bored girlfriends) of golfers stay and get massages and sit by the pool or in the spa.

So we rocked up and sat by the pool, giggling for a while and then . . . well, we just sat there. No one cared. One waiter even brought us some orange juices. And then we went back to the campsite, half elated and half let down by our success, as if we'd been hoping something more would happen. Later – years later – Mum told me that Dad drove on ahead after we walked off down the beach and told them we were coming. He was sitting in the restaurant the whole time we were there, making sure we didn't get into any real trouble. Of course he was the one who arranged our orange juices. I never told Zara or Mieke that. To this day they think those orange juices were on the house, part of the magic of the day.

So now we go every summer and even though Dad doesn't sit in the restaurant any more (I don't know how many years he did that) no one minds us being there. We use the pool and the outdoor spa and have drinks brought to us (but we pay for them ourselves). I guess they know us now or they think we belong, that our dads are playing golf or something.

I wasn't sure we would even go this year. I mean, everything felt weird without Mieke, as if the rules had changed. Would Zara really want to hang out with just me? But when Zara rocked up to my campsite at breakfast and said, 'Are we on?' I knew exactly what she was talking about.

She was wearing these enormous J Lo sunglasses (I could never get away with them) and her hair was perfect – straight and neat and smooth in some kind of twisty up-do thing. I mean, how do you even achieve perfect hair in the wilderness? I was still in my PJs.

'Hi, Zarsparilla.' Teddy crossed her eyes, which is a thing she only does when she likes someone. When she was little it came with a dance.

'Hi, Teddybear Biscuit.'

They're so cute together. Who would have thought Zara could be *cute*?

'You girls breaking into the club?' Mum asked, smiling up at Zara.

'Ooh. My little criminal. I'm so proud,' said Dad.

Teddy made a face. 'Bor-ing,' she said. 'It's all old fogies with tartan pants and floppy hats.'

'What are you guys doing?' I asked. I always feel this pang when I've got plans with friends about being left out of whatever my family is doing, like I wish I could be in two places at once.

'Beach day,' said Mum.

'Dad's going to take me snorkelling at Tallow Beach,' Teddy said.

'Cool. You might find your true family, fish face,' I said, sticking out my tongue.

'Shut up, big bum,' Teddy said back.

Zara gave me a sidelong glance as we walked off, after I'd changed into the one sundress I'd brought with me just for this occasion — Zara still liked us to dress up for the club. 'Doesn't that bother you?' she said, when we were out of earshot.

'Doesn't what bother me?' I asked.

'You know. The fish face, big bum stuff?'

'What? No way. I mean, after all, she does have a fish face, and I do have a big bum.' I waggled it for effect.

'You do not,' said Zara, automatically. She pretty much has no bum.

'Well, it's bigger than yours. Admit it, you're just jealous. You *wish* you had a bum like this.' I waggled again and started singing the big butt song.

We walked up the beach.

'You really don't have a big bum,' Zara said, earnestly.

'Give it up, baby-chil',' I said. 'I don't mind my *ass*,' I said it in an American accent, because 'ass' sounds less rude than 'arse'. I gave it a slap. 'It gives me something comfy to sit on. There's more to life than being super skinny.' As soon as I said that I felt awful. I mean, I wasn't trying to put Zara down or anything. I started to backpedal but Zara just laughed it off.

'Don't worry about it,' Zara said.

But I couldn't help wondering if somewhere under her mask Zara had feelings that could be hurt.

Chapter Five

Zara

How does Tilly do it? She's so sure of herself. She doesn't care about fitting in. She doesn't care about all the millions of rules you have to follow if you want to be popular. She's just herself.

It didn't even seem to bother her that Mieke wasn't here, she'd just adapted straight away. But I didn't have friends like Tilly at school. The smart girls stuck together at my school, they always seemed so intense, always having deep and meaningful conversations and stuff. Sometimes Tilly and Mieke would talk about art or Tilly's philosophy class and I'd just tune out. But without Mieke here, I wasn't sure how to act, what to say. I wasn't sure I got Tilly, not completely. Like for example, she was a crack up, but she poked fun at herself all the time, and laughing felt wrong, like I was poking fun at her too.

We walked up the path to the golf club. I looked out at the beach. It was already starting to get crowded. Soon the water would be full of swimmers, windsurfers, surfers and jet skiers, and little triangle yacht sails out on the horizon. I wished they'd all go away. I wanted the beach for us, for me and Tilly and Mieke. I wanted surf school again, where we owned the beach and nothing else mattered.

For the first time I felt really self-conscious about going to the club, walking up the path — it's kind of bizarre, the difference between two and three. Three is a gang. It gives you more strength to do what you want. Two is like . . . well, it's not that different from one, really. It's vulnerable.

I'm not used to it. Since Jess, since primary school, I haven't had one *best* friend. There's four main girls I hang out with: Kayla, Rio, Sooz and Tang Yi. And then there's another kind of layer below those girls, so there's always a few people around to go shopping with or get a coffee or hang out with at a party or catch a movie.

My mum always said, 'Don't ask, don't tell.' She means secrets. She reckons secrets are *the* currency of popularity. According to her, secrets are what brings girls down. I've seen it happen.

There was this one girl, Ashley. She was all right. But she was a gossip. After she got into the group, she went crazy just knowing all this inside information. She went to Sooz's house to do a project and then told everyone in hushed tones about meeting Sooz's mum who had cancer, talking about her like she was a freak or something because the chemo made her thin and gaunt and bald. She told people about Marie's dad (Marie was on our netball team, she floated between our group and the music kids) who has a restraining order against him and isn't allowed to see his kids but parks outside the school sometimes. She told people who liked who, who was dumping who, who was bitching about who . . . it was pretty much stuff we all knew, but it wasn't cool to spread it around outside the group. And plus she said some stuff that Kayla had said about Rio being slutty at Sooz's birthday party – ouch. Kayla and Rio didn't speak for days. But then we, well Kayla, decided to punish Ashley. We froze her out. She cornered us individually, saying, 'But what did I do? Just tell me what I did?' After about a week all the girls stood round her on the oval at lunchtime and Kayla asked, in this really hurt tone, 'Just tell us *why*. Why did you do it?' Ashley was a mess in minutes. As if there's an acceptable answer. Ashley has a bunch of new friends now, nobodies really. I don't think any of them like her much either.

Anyway, I don't ever tell anyone else's secrets, and I don't ask to know them. I don't even *want* to know really, but if someone wants to tell me stuff, I'll listen. In fact, it's amazing how many people *have* told me stuff – I guess 'cause they know I won't tell. I don't tell my own secrets either. Like, I don't tell anyone about Mum and Dad and how they don't talk and that I'm scared they don't love each other, or how my dad doesn't talk to me anymore and I'm scared he doesn't love me either. I never told anyone about the time Marcus and I nearly . . . you know. And I didn't tell *anyone* about the night of the party, the last week of school, about walking in on Marcus . . . or about the stuff that happened afterwards. Don't ask. Don't tell.

So I'm popular. And I have these four friends. But Rio and Tang Yi, they hang out all the time. And Sooz and Kayla are totally BFF, they have been since kindergarten. So even though I'm popular, even though most people think I'm, like, *it*, sometimes I look at my friends and think . . . well. They don't know me at all. Sometimes I'm surrounded by people and I'm completely alone. 'Cause I might be the most popular girl in the school, but you know what? No one likes me the best. Boohoo, right? Poor little Miss Popular. Now that's a secret I'm definitely not telling.

I love the golf club. Maybe there is some of my mother in me after all. I'd die if she heard me say that. But I love the blue-tiled lap pool with the fake waterfall and the spa, the waiters who walk past and get you drinks. I like the fake Bali huts. Even the sun feels extra luxurious here, you know? I love that my sunglasses cover half my face like a movie star's, like I'm incognito. I love that they put little umbrellas into the drinks.

'Hey, they've been recruiting,' hissed Tilly.

I glanced around without sitting up on my deckchair. 'Yeah, I guess,' I said.

'Come on, you can't say you haven't noticed!'

'Since when did you get boy crazy?' I asked Tilly. 'You sound like you're thirteen.'

'I don't know. It had to happen sometime. And there are some seriously manic-state-inducing specimens here.'

'I guess.' Actually, Tilly was right. There were three or four new waiters, all about our age, all pretty buff looking. Maybe it was a new service to the golf widows, all those rich lonely women. A couple of the new recruits were standing together now and whispering to each other, looking at us.

One of them came over. 'Are you girls supposed to be here?' he asked. 'The pool is for guests of the resort and club members only.'

Tilly looked at me. We've *never* been challenged at the golf club. I sat up. I felt this tingle come over me. And then I spoke.

'Don't you *know* who we are?' I demanded. Tilly's mouth dropped open. The guy looked uncomfortable and glanced over at Tilly. I took off my sunglasses. 'I'd like to see your manager. Now.'

'Zara,' Tilly hissed. I frowned at her and turned my attention back to the recruit. He opened his mouth to say something but I started up again before he had a chance.

'We have been coming to this resort for years,' I said. 'We have a long history here. I think the resort would be very sorry to lose our custom, and our parents',' I emphasised. 'Now,' I waved my hand and saw Tilly munching on her palm to stop herself from laughing, 'two cokes, please. *With* fresh lemon.'

'Lemon?'

'All the European resorts put lemon in their cokes,' I said, putting my sunglasses back on. I was wearing the Botox-bored face. It's a great way to deal with people in the service industry. I know. I work in it – my title, get this, is coffee maid. I half expect to be asked to do it topless.

As he walked away, Tilly rolled over and pressed her face into the deckchair's pillow. She let out a muffled squeal.

'You were brilliant,' she said, rolling her head over and peeking out at me. 'But do you think they're going to kick us out?'

'I don't know,' I admitted. 'But I feel like we do have a right to be here. More right than the transient soon-to-be-divorced golf widows. We've got a history, dammit.'

'You go, girl. Self-righteous indignation is your specialty. I can't believe how much guts you've got.' Tilly's eyes twinkled. 'For such a skinny-ass chick.'

'Thanks!' My mobile chimed and I jumped. 'Sorry. Message.' I rummaged around in my bag, feeling slightly ill, the way I always did now when a text came through. But it was just Sooz.

Tilly looked past me. 'Crap, he's coming back,' Tilly squawked. 'And – *crap!* – he's got the manager.'

'Be cool,' I said, not looking up.

I checked my message. *Hey Zara. We're on! See you next week. Sooz.* Next week? I'd still be in Indigo next week. She was obviously confused. Sooz was often confused.

Then I remembered The Plan. They were coming down this way in a few days, staying at nearby Alder Springs. How could I have forgotten The Plan? They'd come and get me, I'd go back with them, one long party. Yeah, right. I was about to text Sooz back, wondering how I would get out of it, when I noticed Tilly was definitely not cool. I dropped my mobile back in my bag.

The manager came over, looking harassed. But I was kind of into this. I didn't even mind being kicked out. I mean, we've only been waiting for it for like eight years. I just wished Mieke could have been here to see it.

But then the manager, Mr Whitehouse, grinned. 'Hi, girls. You know you're welcome here. Anything they want, on the house,' he said to the waiter. 'Where's your friend?'

'She's coming next week,' Tilly said, relieved, grinning cheekily at the waiter.

'Oh, well, bring her up when she does. Say hi to your dad for me,' he said to Tilly as he left.

I glared at the waiter who'd tried to kick us out. 'You heard him.'

'Cokes with lemon,' the waiter said. He looked annoyed and amused all at once. He glanced at Tilly again, who covered her mouth apologetically as if she was trying not to laugh, and went to get our cokes.

'*We* go, girl,' I said to Tilly and she did laugh this time, her head back, a big open-throated laugh.

Chapter Six
Tilly

The cute waiter brought us our drinks. 'So, since you girls are like best buds with the manager, are you coming to Tank on Friday night?'

'What's Tank?' I asked. Zara didn't look up.

'It's a venue at the clubhouse after the restaurant closes. The music's great, they get DJs down from Melbourne and Sydney and they have these totally random themes. Last week it was Aquarium. One guy came as one of those dudes with the heavy helmet thing, the ones you get in the bottom of fishtanks. He even danced in it. This week it's Secret Identities. Clark Kent, Diana Prince, Wally West.'

'Who?' said Zara.

'Superman, Wonder Woman, The Flash,' I supplied.

He looked impressed. 'Very good. No one guesses Wally West.' He flashed a disarming grin in my direction. Then he looked from me back to Zara. 'So are you coming?'

I didn't say anything. I mean, it was obviously Zara he was inviting. I doubt he cared if I came or not.

'Sounds okay,' Zara said, looking the other way.

'Cool. I'm Andrew, by the way, but all my friends call me Sawyer.'

'As in the guy from that freaky show *Lost*?' Zara asked.

'As in Tom.'

'From the book?' I said. See, I always ask the cutting questions.

'That's right.'

Sexy *and* bookish? Hold me back.

'I'm Tilly,' I said. 'This is Zara.'

'Are you girls staying at the resort?' he asked me.

'Nah. We camp at the foreshore every year.'

'Really?' Sawyer said, as though he didn't quite believe us.

'What?' Zara said grumpily. I could tell she wanted him to disappear. But I didn't.

'Let's just say the girls I know who look like you don't go camping,' Sawyer said.

At least he included both of us in that statement, though I knew he meant Zara. Okay, he was stupid to say it, but look, to be honest, it wasn't completely an unfair call. The girl who's the Zara, the top alpha, at our school? Her name's Cleo Macintyre. She'd die if she knew I was saying this, but she used to be my best friend back in primary school. We used to grub around in the dirt together down by the creek, setting traps for fairies and making these elaborate bee-catchers with sticks, leaves and mashed up flowers and honey (they never worked). Anyway, pretty much the day she turned twelve, she developed a serious allergy to dirt and to anything that involved exerting herself more than lifting a mobile phone to her ear. Talking to me, for example, acknowledging my existence? Yeah, that was a bit too strenuous.

But Zara looked offended. 'Who asked you?' she said to Sawyer.

I got into conflict-resolution mode – I hate confrontation. 'I know I *look* really delicate,' I said. 'But that's just the price of being beautiful. Sometimes I have to slum it. You know, to see what the unbeautiful people are doing. I mean, you never know when you're going to have a hideous accident and wake up unbeautiful yourself. Or, worse, get a pimple. I have to be prepared for all possibilities.'

Sawyer stared at me. He tilted his head as if he was really looking at me.

'It could happen,' I said, unnerved.

'To you?' he said, and now he was looking right into my eyes. I suddenly wished I was wearing Zara's enormous sunglasses. 'Never.'

I know he was carrying on the joke. But my insides went squoosh and my nether regions went zing. Squoosh and zing. I'm sure everyone at the whole resort heard it.

I couldn't sit still, not with him looking at me like that. I stood up. 'Anyone want another drink?' I asked.

'Um, I'm like, your waiter,' Sawyer said.

Even Zara was staring at me as if I was a complete freak. From underneath her sunglasses, but I knew she was.

'Oh yeah, I'm . . .' I waved my hand vaguely, and suddenly I had to get away. I walked off, still dazed and confused. Luckily I found myself outside the ladies toilets so I went in and consulted the mirror. Still pointy. My face I mean. Nothing had changed. I wasn't suddenly a beautiful sex goddess. My hair was coming out of its ponytail – that's what happens when you have frizzy hair. Go anywhere near the beach or out in the rain or in humid weather and your hair comes alive and starts threatening to take prisoners.

Sawyer was – no kidding – rock god material. The kind of slightly alternative rock that you like until you catch your mum humming along to it in the car. He had this lazy sexy smile, and these eyes, dark and fringed with beautiful lashes. I could run my fingers through those lashes. So why was he looking at *me* like that? Zing, zing and zing.

But when I came out of the toilets and saw he was looking at Zara with those fringed, dark eyes, I felt the familiar sagging disappointment that came with resignation. Of course it wasn't me he was interested in. He was just a flirt. Some guys are like that. You know, they come up to you outside English class, look you in the eye, call you by your name and for a moment it's like you're the only person in the world, until the next, prettier girl comes along.

'Yeah, so it's a great night. You and Tilly should totally come,' he was saying to Zara. 'You can watch the surf, you know how the club's floodlights shine out on the water after dark? Well, with the music and everything, it's just, like . . . another world.'

Zara's interest finally piqued. 'Floodlights? Oh, yeah. Down on the beach. I'd forgotten they did that.'

I sat back down again. The conversation dried up. 'So, those drinks?' Sawyer offered.

Because I was the one who mentioned them, I had to nod, even though I really didn't want him to go.

We had another coke each and then, after hanging out a little bit longer, watching Sawyer turn those eyes on every golf widow in the joint, we left. I was buzzing on caffeine and sugar as we walked up the beach.

'He was nice,' I said. 'Didn't you think he was nice?'

'Mmm,' Zara said, distractedly, looking out at the water.

'Do you want to go?' I asked eagerly.

'Where?' Zara said, quickly, looking at me almost suspiciously. Sometimes she's just weird. Maybe it was the caffeine making her edgy. 'Oh, you mean like the nightclub thing.'

'Yeah yeah yeah!' Buzz buzz buzz.

She shrugged. 'It's something to do.'

'Yay!' I didn't mention the dressing up thing, in case she thought it was lame and changed her mind. But I did have to run in one big circle with my arms out pretending to be a plane. Come on, all that caffeine and sugar rushing through my body? It had to burn off somehow.

Zara laughed. 'He *was* cute, I suppose,' she said finally, poking me in the arm when I ended up back beside her.

I bounded like a puppy. 'He *was*, wasn't he.' But what goes up must come down. Maybe it was the low after my sugar high, but I felt my stomach – and my expectations – drop. 'I think he really liked you,' I said.

Zara snorted. 'He's not my type.'

That's injustice, isn't it? I liked him, he liked her, and she couldn't even be bothered with him.

'Why not? He's gorgeous,' I said. Why was I trying to talk her into him?

'You should totally go for it,' Zara said.

'Yeah, right.'

'I'm serious.'

'Like I've got a chance.'

'Well, you won't if you put yourself down all the time.'

I just shrugged. I was feeling really blue now. Deep blue. Cobalt. Navy.

'Guys are . . . you know. They don't *care* what you look like,' Zara said. 'They're just animals. They follow the hormones.'

If it was meant to be reassuring, it wasn't. Was she saying if they did care what girls looked like, I wouldn't have a chance? And hey, since when did guys not care what girls looked like?

Zara looked at my face and said, exasperated, 'Sometimes you're so dumb for someone who's so smart. It's pheromones. It's chemistry. You know, like science. You have to be a match. Guys don't care who the prettiest girl in the room is or who the smartest girl is. You just have to smell right.'

'Are you freaking kidding me?'

'It's science,' Zara said. 'Science doesn't lie.'

'Science? Or did you get this from a perfume advertorial.'

Zara thought about it. 'Okay. Maybe it *was* from an advertorial. But it makes sense, right?'

I laughed and kicked sand at her.

'Right?' she said.

Chapter Seven
Zara

As soon as Sawyer mentioned the floodlights, like in that very second, a whole detailed plan was born in my head. It was a freaking *eureka* moment, you know, like that dude in the bath?

So that's why I was there, scrabbling about in the pitch dark with the beach-box lock at eleven o'clock at night. 'Cause guess what? Turns out you can't unlock a padlock in one hand while holding a tiny torch in the other. Even if it's a Maglight torch that can be run over by a Mack truck, which apparently they can. Tilly told me.

I tried burying the torch in the sand, pointing at the lock, but the sand was too soft and it didn't work. So I turfed the torch and did it by feel. There was a streetlight behind the beach boxes so it wasn't completely dark, but it was shining right in my eyes, so it wasn't helping either. Finally I got the door open. Everything was wedged in tight and it took me a while to work my surfboard out of the clutter. Mine's the pink one, of course. My mum is obsessed with pink. It's kind of grotesque in a grown woman. It was bad enough when I was four. Seriously. But every bike, every doll, every dress my mum has ever bought me has featured the colour pink in some kind of garish way. When I move out of home, I plan to burn every pink thing I own.

Except maybe my surfboard.

I left the torch at the beach box and walked up the beach, surfboard under my arm towards the golf club floodlights. Was I crazy, wandering around alone on the beach at night? Were there murderers and rapists lurking in the shadowy bushes? To be honest, I didn't care. I didn't really care about anything. Why didn't I care? Was it part of the bored face? Could something inside me freeze too, could your *heart* freeze when the wind changed?

Well anyway, if there were murderers and rapists in the bushes, the sight of a girl struggling up the beach with a pink surfboard (okay, so it was night and they probably couldn't see it was pink) must have been, I don't know, offputting or something because they stayed in the bushes. I walked towards the golf club, which was lit up like a beacon in the dunes. The lights shone straight out onto the sea, reflecting against the dark surface and illuminating the white crests of the waves. I kicked off my scuffs, hoping

I'd be able to find them again. I had my rashie and board-shorts on already, so after putting on my ankle strap and making sure it was attached to the board, I waded out into the water. The air was warm and balmy and even the sea felt as if it retained the heat of the day. I pushed myself out, holding onto the board, paddling forward. The tides are strong at Indigo, which is part of what makes it so popular. It's considered a safe surf beach (during the day, in good weather, when the beach is patrolled), though Chris, the guy who taught surf school, was quick to point out that there's no such thing as safe surfing.

'If there was,' he said with a grin, 'we wouldn't do it. The fact that there's consequences — dire consequences — that's the rush.'

That's what I was thinking about as I dived under the first wave, holding the board. Consequences.

It took me a while to get the rhythm of paddling. It was strange to be on a surfboard again, but good too. It felt . . . you know, right. I could hear my own breathing. A couple of times the board bobbed out from under me, or a rolling wave tipped me off. But after a while I stopped fighting it and remembered to move with the board. It's when you try and keep it still, try to act like you're on solid ground, that it beats you.

It was weird paddling out into the darkness. I was fighting my own instincts just to keep going. The part of me that's wired for survival wanted me to turn around now, put the surfboard away, go back to my cosy tent and zip myself in. But pushing against this instinct felt good, like getting on a rollercoaster. Or when you're abseiling, that moment where you jump into the abyss. I felt this crazy joy hammering against my ribcage.

I could see enough to see the crests of the waves coming towards me. I got out beyond the break and rested, waiting for my first wave. I stretched the muscles in my shoulders and arms. They were still warming up, they already felt tight and sore from paddling, but the pain was the good kind.

The water was a black sheet, all surface. Anything could be under there, swirling around in the darkness. I felt myself getting spooked as I waited for something to happen. I was nerve and muscle, ready to leap. A wave started to build, heading towards me. As I felt the board rise, I turned around, paddling, getting ready to stand up.

But the instant I turned around I was hit by the golf club lights burning the back of my eyeballs. A thousand fragments of light sprayed in front of me, disorienting me. As the wave lifted me I lost my nerve, hanging back at the last minute. The churning sea tossed me off the board and I went under. My eyes were open as I pushed against the wave, but in the darkness I had to guess which way was up. It wasn't till I jarred my head on the sandy bottom that I realised I'd guessed wrong. The cord on my ankle pulled tight and my leg yanked up as my board bobbed onto the surface with me following it.

I was scared now, I admit it. Suddenly I realised how

dangerous this was. It wasn't like abseiling, where you've got harnesses and ropes and helmets to stop you if you fall, so it's just an exercise of the mind, the danger minimal. Out here, tonight, there was nothing, no safety net, no anchor. The waves felt huge in the dark. I was going to have to do this by feel if I wanted to catch a wave. My head ached a bit where I'd whacked it and I was tempted to swim in, call it quits. But something made me stay. I paddled out and waited for another wave, and as I saw one build, I turned again, my eyes half shut. I felt the wave as it lifted, and when I was sure I was at the top of it, I stood.

The feeling of catching that wave, of pushing through the black water, my eyes adjusting so I could follow the curl of the water . . . I wish I had more words. I wish I had Tilly's words. It was like I was the only person in the world. It was like I was part of the night sky. It was amazing. I felt this joy well up inside me, pushing out through my chest. I felt more lit up than the golf club. I was so pure. It wasn't like flying. It was like . . . like nothing I could explain. Everything was heightened by the night. The waves were bigger and I seemed to be faster, I skimmed the surface of the ocean as if I was *made* of light.

I could feel the whole sea flowing up, through the board, into me. My body was the meeting point of sea and sky. My body *and* the board, meshed together: fibreglass and skin, wax, sweat, saltwater. And in the middle of it all, in the midst of movement and action and energy, my mind felt perfectly calm. Like how inside a cyclone everything is meant to be peaceful and still. I was lit up. I was glowing.

It was unreal. As in not real. It was a dream ride. The best kind.

Of course I fell off the board, backwards, straight onto my bum, breaking through the surface of the water. But that didn't make it less of a dream. This time I just relaxed under the water, enjoying the feeling of it as it enclosed me, letting myself plummet then rise. I let my board tug me upwards. I popped out of the water and hauled myself back onto the surfboard. I lay there panting. Suddenly I was really, really tired. My bones were tired. My arms felt heavy. I could have closed my eyes on that board and slept. Except now that I was wet the warm sea air was starting to feel chilly. At the same time a warm peace flooded through me, an afterglow.

I paddled back to the shore. My skin was buzzing, I felt electric – maybe it was the cold, maybe it was something else, some leftover joy. I found my shoes and carried the board back to the beach box and stowed it. Man, I was knackered, in a good way. Getting rid of the board lightened me up a bit and I walked back to the campsite, swinging my arms in the cold wind and just trying to get a bit of circulation back. I'd stashed my towel and some PJs in the girls shower before I went – see what I mean about the plan being detailed? – so I had a hot shower and dressed quickly, rubbing my hair dry in front of the mirror before collapsing into my tent. I thought I'd be asleep before my head touched down but I lay awake, staring out at the world and living it again — being on that surfboard, upright, balancing under a night sky — over and over in my head, like it was a movie, seeing it like I was somewhere above, outside myself, looking down.

Chapter Eight
Tilly

Zara wasn't up when I went down to her tent. Usually Zara was the first awake, groomed and gorgeous before the rest of us had faced our soggy cereal, so it was weird that she was still asleep.

I drifted aimlessly away from her campsite. Every year when we came to Indigo I spent some of the time with Zara and Mieke and some of the time with my mum and dad and Teddy. And some time just hanging out on my own. So it wasn't like I didn't know what to do with myself. But I was restless, waiting for something to happen. As if something had a hold of me and was pulling me through summer, a huge gravity machine or a giant magnet. It was like a dream: I was looking for something – but what?

I heard heavy footsteps behind me crunching the gravel, as if someone was running up the path. I turned around.

'Tilly, I thought that was you,' Ivan said, panting.

'Yep.' Well, it *was* me. What else could I have said?

'I was wondering . . . are you busy?'

'Um, no.'

'Do you want to come for a walk?'

Okay. Now if a boy asked you to come for a walk at breakfast o'clock, after you died of shock and everything, you'd think he probably meant a stroll down by the beach, a bit of a chat, maybe end up getting a coffee somewhere. Am I right?

Half an hour later we were rounding the headland at Point Block (isn't that just the best name? I love a good oxymoron). We hadn't spoken more than two words because Ivan had exactly two gears: lightspeed and supersonic. I was going to be the first person to die of a brisk walk. I was panting hard and must have been bright red all over (I can't blush, but I turn into a beetroot when you combine me with exercise – I can't win.) My *hair* was sweating.

'Shall we sit down?' Ivan said, gesturing at a flat rock.

I have never sat so fast in my life. Hello, rock. I love you, rock.

'Are you all right?' Ivan asked me, looking at me funny. He perched on the other end. 'Sorry, I didn't realise you were struggling. You should have told me to slow down.'

'Couldn't . . . speak . . .' I gasped, willing my face to return to its usual freckle-splotch-and-putty colour.

'Sorry,' Ivan said again, leaning forward and staring

intently into his backpack. 'I've got chocolate somewhere. And water.'

'Water first.' I gulped down half the bottle before accepting some chocolate. The chocolate was hard and sweet in my mouth, like manna from heaven. I sucked on a square while I looked at Ivan rummaging around in his backpack for another water bottle (scared of girl germs, obviously).

It suddenly occurred to me that I was in the middle of the wilderness with a boy. What was I doing here? Was I completely stark raving? I mean, why had he brought me so far away from humanity?

'I wanted to talk to you, actually,' Ivan said.

'Mmm?' I asked, mouth full of chocolate and seized with cold fear that was more about being alone with a boy than about Ivan being a potential sex-crazed, axe-wielding lunatic. Well, for a start, no axe.

'It's about Zara.'

Oh.

'Because you're about the only one of her friends who isn't a complete loser.'

Okaaay. Is that one of those back-handed insults? I'm a loser but not a complete loser? So does that mean I'm a *failed* loser?

He must have read my facial expression because he said, 'Sorry, I didn't mean that the way it sounded. But you seem like a together kind of girl . . .'

I'm pretty sure he meant frumpy. You know, like when

teachers call you 'a sensible girl' and what they mean is you have no friends and spend all lunchtime volunteering to re-catalogue books in the library.

'. . . and, well, I'm worried about her.'

'You're worried about Zara?' I asked, thinking it was probably about time I aimed for a sentence. Spoken out loud. 'She seems okay to me.'

'She's so . . . disconnected. There's something going on with her. I thought maybe —' Ivan wasn't looking at *me*, by the way. He was staring at his hands, at his feet, out at the water, anywhere but at me. 'I thought maybe she was taking drugs.'

'Are you serious? Zara?' I said. 'No way.'

Look, I live in the inner city. I see drugs around. I have several funny junkies-on-the-street stories. Heaps of the kids at school have tried weed; some smoke it more than others. (Not me. I'm self-righteous, remember? I don't even drink alcohol. You can't be the boss if you've got spew in your hair, so therefore getting drunk holds little or no appeal to me.) Occasionally someone in the toilets at the school social claims to be selling ecstasy, but it's nearly always cat worming pills. Some poor sucker dances under the disco ball waving her arms around saying, 'I can taste the colours.' Most girls I know can't afford drugs anyway — do you know how much lattes and magazines and iTunes and prepaid and library fines cost these days? Face it, all our parents are running around wetting their pants that we're chroming or on ice and some of us are still trying to get up the nerve to ask a boy out. Well, not Zara, obviously. But me, for example.

Which brings us back to Ivan. Did he really lure me all the way out into the bush to talk about Zara? How disappointing.

'Okay,' he was saying, 'maybe it's not drugs. But *something* is going on with her. Could you at least . . . keep an eye on her?'

Was he asking me to spy on her? 'And report back to you?'

'Oh no, no,' Ivan said, as if shocked at the thought. 'You don't have to do that. I just thought she might be more likely to confide in you. She really likes you, Tilly. She's a different person in Indigo, with you and Mieke around. The girls she hangs out with at school . . .' Ivan made a face.

I was grinning but I tried to turn it into a modest smile. I was flattered that Ivan said Zara liked me so much. I was also flattered by his insinuation that Mieke and I were somehow superior to her other friends.

And hey, how sweet was Ivan? His concern for Zara was making him look all furrowed, like this old teddy bear I had at home. Some of his fur kept stubbornly going in the wrong direction, no matter how much you stroked him. I wanted to reach out and stroke Ivan, actually. I was suddenly really physically aware of him, sitting there. I mean, here we were, on either end of a broad flat rock, an arm's length from each other . . . We were quiet for a moment and I thought, maybe this was it. Maybe this was what I'd been waiting for. I had this sudden fantasy of throwing myself at him, mashing my lips against his, his hand clasping the back of my neck, kissing me back harder.

I was pulled out of my fantasy when Ivan stood up, and I leapt up too, embarrassed that he might have read my thoughts. He stopped to put the water bottles into the backpack and reluctantly I turned to walk back down the path. But Ivan lingered, looking out through the trees. 'I love it here,' he said, surprising me.

I'd been too out of breath to even notice the view when we arrived. I realised you could see all of Indigo Bay on one side and all of Tallow Beach, which is quieter and more sheltered, on the other side. We were high above both, and for a moment it gave me the feeling of being a seagull, about to soar up into the wind. I nearly said that to Ivan, but it seemed kind of dumb so I decided to conserve my energy for the sprint back to the campsite.

We settled into a pace somewhere between normal and lightspeed, which, compared to the walk up, felt quite leisurely. At least I could think.

Zara did seem a bit . . . something. Not like she was on drugs – Ivan was way off on that count, I was sure of it. But still, she'd been particularly quiet this year, sort of reserved about her life, maybe a bit on edge. I mean, I had nothing particularly special to report because I'm a big geeky nerd who doesn't do anything, but usually Zara mentions boyfriends or her friends or parties she's been to (I know, because I hang vicariously off every word) and she hasn't done that at all. Yesterday on the way back from the golf club she'd seemed kind of distracted; I thought it was weird at the time. And then the uncharacteristic sleep-in this morning . . . so maybe Ivan did have a real reason to be concerned about Zara. Part of me thrilled at the thought. It felt like I was peering in through a crack in the wardrobe door, into that other world — Zara's world. I wanted drama. I wanted action. I wanted insight.

As we walked the steeply sloping path to the beach, I looked down at the top of Ivan's head. You know phrenology, when people used to read the bumps in the head to determine personality traits? Well, I had a lot of time to read the crown of Ivan's head. His hair was cropped very short, like a military style haircut. I remember a few years ago, when it was longer, gold, a little bit woolly, with soft curls. I wonder if he cut it short to make himself look more serious, more adult. He did look serious, all the time. A slight frown always seemed to pucker between his eyebrows. It was kind of sexy, in a brooding, inaccessible way. I couldn't help comparing Ivan to Sawyer, the cute waiter. There was an openness about Sawyer, a sense that he was up for anything, on the lookout for mischief. It was as if Sawyer was the opposite of Ivan. Who would I choose, if I had a choice? What did I want from a boyfriend? Brooding, intense and serious, or fun and flirty and up for a laugh?

I sighed. Zara was right. I was Tilly Dove, boy crazy. Crazy being the operative word.

Chapter Nine

Zara

Mum woke me with a cup of coffee and vegemite on toast cut into soldiers, like I was a kid.

I rubbed my eyes, peering up at her through the mesh of the swag. 'What time is it?'

'Half past nine.'

I groaned and tried to bury my head back in my swag. But now that I was awake I could feel the dry heat of the morning sun; my swag was like a sauna. I crawled out and accepted the coffee and toast. I carried them over to the table under the gazebo adjacent to our caravan, an open tent-like thing where we eat all our meals. Mum and Dad have all these complicated systems for camping, basically to fool Mum into thinking she's not really camping at all.

'I recharged your phone!' Mum called from the caravan. When I didn't respond, she brought it out. 'Don't you want it? Goodness, I thought you couldn't live without it.'

'Of course I can live without it,' I muttered as Mum dropped it into my lap.

'I was only trying to help,' Mum said. 'I thought you might be missing your friends.'

Sometimes I think Mum likes my friends more than I do. She's always going on about how popular she was. To Mum being popular is the most important thing in the world. More important than the environment or world peace, as if there's nothing more to life. I mean, nobody wants to be alone. Not at school, anyway. But somehow, as I get older, it seems . . . I don't know. Like there's more. Like there should be more.

I turned my phone on. It was funny how different it felt to me now. Before I always kept my phone on me. It was part of me. I had fuzzy charms that Sooz had given me and this totally cute crocheted cover with seashell buttons – Tang Yi made one for each of us for Christmas last year. I had ringtones I'd downloaded with my friends and photos of us all stored in the memory. Everyone I knew was programmed into my address book. At home my phone was my salvation. It was a tunnel, a telescope, my view to the outside world, my escape, my protection from my worst nightmare: being alone with my family.

But now it felt like, instead of my way out, it was someone else's way in.

There were a few messages from Sooz. She had a habit of SMSing her thought of the minute, for instance: *ur totally missing Veronica Mars. Logan is 2 hot.* And: *tell me not to eat anymore peppermint santas omigosh I'm so addicted.*

The last one ended with *cu in Indigo.* I still hadn't returned her last message.

I don't even know why I read the other message, because just seeing those words — number withheld — made me feel sick. But somehow I couldn't stop myself. It said: *You know you want it Zara.*

Whatever. Whatever. I deleted it. I deleted Sooz's messages too and buried my phone deep in my backpack.

I pulled out shorts and a sports bra. I was stiff from surfing. I'm pretty fit but surfing must use different muscles or something, or maybe I'd worked harder than I thought, struggling against the waves to get back out there, to start again. I walked down to the beach and found a quiet place to do some yoga stretches. I couldn't focus. I don't know if it was the text message, but I felt invaded, my skin was crawling, as if I was being watched. I tried to shake it off, but I couldn't.

So I ran instead, along the sand, barefoot, right at the water's edge, the sea refreshingly cold as it lapped at my feet. But I still couldn't run that grubby little text message away. That's what made me angry. I'm strong, right? I'm no fighter, but if he was standing right in front of me, I'd punch him, I'd push him down onto the sand, I'd rub his face into it. But how do you fight words?

I thought back to the night at Kayla's party, the night Marcus and I broke up. Well, kind of broke up. He'd led me up the stairs to Kayla's bedroom. We sat on the bed and kissed. Sometimes, when we were alone like that, he got pushy, he was kind of rough. Sometimes if he'd been drinking he'd try to go further, jamming his hands into the waistband of my jeans or sliding it up my top. He said, 'Other girls do it.' He was probably right. Part of me thought I should too, get it over with. But I always pulled away.

Anyway, that night, he wasn't pushy. He kissed me for a while and I kissed him back. I must have tasted like vodka. He tasted sickeningly sweet, like lawn clippings, and he smelt like smoke. The warm fuzziness of the alcohol was wearing off. I had a headache starting and every time I closed my eyes the room started to spin. I just wanted to lie down and close my eyes. He must have sensed my reluctance because he pulled back and moaned, 'Oh Zara, what are you doing to me?'

No, I didn't want to think about that. Because when I thought about Marcus, I thought about later, about walking in on him with her — and about the look on Marcus's face, the blank smile, the narrow slitted eyes.

So as I ran, I thought about Tang Yi instead, how that night we'd danced like we were fourteen again. We were silly and brave, trying out crazy hip-hop steps, doing fake karaoke, pretending we were famous, not caring if anyone was watching. Sooz and Rio joined us, we lined up and did the Bus Stop, and it was like it used to be, before we started having boyfriends or drinking or any of that stuff.

It was after that night the text messages began.

I picked up the speed, pushing against the wet sand as I ran.

I concentrated on my body's movement, the long, taut muscles in my thighs and the stringy muscles down the back of my calves. I thought about the way the body fits together, all the cogs and joints, the cartilage and ligaments we studied in health class, and how they make our bodies flexible, make it possible to run, dance, surf. I pushed myself harder, feeling the resistance of the sand under my feet. My lungs were bursting, but I knew I could push through it, push through the pain. There was a point I knew I could get myself to, eventually, if I just kept thrashing myself, where I could run forever. The pain dulls into nothing, and the body just seems to propel itself like a gliding bird, like travelling in a car on a rainy day with slow music — inside you feel slow, even though outside the rushing world is nothing but a blur.

I was almost through the pain when I saw Dad fishing off the rocks. He was looking out at the water. What did *he* see when he looked at the ocean? Did he see huge and impressive, or blank and empty?

I lost my stride. My feet staggered to a stop and I leaned forward, panting. Then I turned around and ran back up the beach, away from Dad, trying to leave my memories behind too.

When darkness came and Mum and Dad and Ivan were sleeping, I went surfing again.

As I paddled out, that instinct was there again, telling me to turn back, to stay where it was light and warm and safe. But I pushed it away, literally, pushing the water back with my arms. Last night's muscles were tight and sore, but they loosened as I swam.

I got the rhythm of the waves faster this time. I thought about blind people, how their other senses evolve and sharpen to compensate for their lost sight. So as I turned to paddle to the top of the wave, I closed my eyes, so the light wouldn't take me by surprise, and to remind myself that I needed to do this by feel. The waves on the sandbar were rougher, choppier than the previous night's and I had trouble staying upright. But finally I caught one and it was a real smooth ride. I crouched down and with my hands touching the board I cut right into it. I opened my eyes. I was in a dark, low tunnel. After the arduous journey out into the water, dragging myself and the board against the current time and time again with every missed wave, the ride itself was bliss. The floodlights from the golf club bounced around inside, scattering into little pieces of light. Last night I'd felt part of the sea; tonight I was weightless, I was air, I was the tunnel, the darkness that rolled under the wave. I was part of the space between water, part of the nothing, the unknown.

At the shoreline, in the darkness, Tilly was waiting for me. To be honest she scared the crap out of me. I'd stood up and was hanging onto my board when I saw this figure looming.

'Tilly?'

As I got closer, I saw her face was tight and grim, staring me down as if she thought I'd gone for good or something, as if she thought I'd gone into the water to drown myself.

'You followed me?' I said. I felt like a little kid who'd been caught doing something bad. But I was also curious.

Tilly nodded.

'Why?'

She looked away. Then met my eyes. 'I guess I wanted to know where you were going,' she said, which was an answer and not an answer. Usually Tilly is straight up, you know? Maybe it's why I like her so much – she's not into secrets.

We were both standing ankle deep in the water. My legs were like jelly. Tilly had a sarong wrapped around her shoulders but I could see her giving the occasional shiver.

But maybe it wasn't the cold that was making her shiver. She looked like she was going to yell at me for doing something dangerous. But she didn't. Suddenly she said, all in a rush, not loudly but with urgency, almost painfully, 'I want to do it too.' I glanced behind me at the sea when she said it, as if to say, 'What, this?' But I knew what she meant, even though I couldn't believe she was saying it. It was like she *knew* what it meant to be riding waves under the night sky, like she understood without me even telling her. It was freezing, but I was beyond cold. So was Tilly. She looked past me, out at the black sea. 'I want to do it,' she said again. She didn't even sound like Tilly. She sounded older and . . . hungry.

'Next time,' I said, and my voice came out low and gravelly, though I meant it to be gentle. 'I'll come get you, okay?' When I said it, I meant it. I wanted to share it, to let someone else inside my skin, to feel what I felt. But I regretted it straight away, because deep down I knew it couldn't be shared. It was all about being alone out there, truly, absolutely alone. Maybe by telling Tilly she could come, I'd just lost it, whatever it was.

As we walked back towards the campground, my body was still buzzing from the surf. Talking about it would change it, but since Tilly was silent, I didn't mind the company. Maybe it would be all right after all, if she understood.

Tilly left me at the toilet block when I went in for my shower. Each of us was alone in the darkness. I wondered how long it took Tilly to fall asleep.

The next morning while I was eating breakfast, Ivan dropped my phone on the table in front of me.

'Have you been going through my bag?' I asked. The big freak.

'I found it on the ground. It must have fallen out.'

I pushed it away a bit. 'Whatever.'

Ivan looked at me carefully. 'Aren't you going to check it?'

'Why's everyone so freaking concerned about my text messages all of a sudden?' I snapped.

'I don't know. Is there a reason we should be?'

Had he been reading my messages? No way. But why was he looking at me like that?

'Fine,' I said. I checked the messages, looking at him pointedly as I jabbed the buttons to get into the menu. There were heaps. One from Kayla, three from Sooz, and a couple from the other girls at school. And one from my creepy new best friend, Number Withheld.

But it was the last one, from Marcus, that caught my eye. *Hey Z, we need 2 talk. Pls call me. I miss you.* I stared at it. I hadn't heard from Marcus since Kayla's party.

The party. I was supposed to be staying at Kayla's that night, but then Tang Yi offered me a lift home with her boyfriend, and I thought about being away from the noise and throng of the party, in the quiet of my own room, slipping between cool, comfortable sheets. I went up to Kayla's bedroom to get my bag.

I walked right in on them, totally unsuspecting. Marcus and Kayla. She was kneeling by the bed, her face at his crotch. He had her head in his hands and he had this look on his face, this spaced out, switched off, nothing look. He opened his eyes, looked at me, and smiled. There was a flatness, a blankness to that smile, to his slitted eyes, to the flat planes of his face. I backed out of the room before Kayla could turn around. She didn't see me. As far as I know she still doesn't know that I was there. I haven't seen or talked to Marcus since. He tried to call a few times but I never answered his calls, and after a while he gave up.

Ivan was staring at me. 'What are you looking at?' I leapt up. 'There's no bloody privacy around here.' I stalked off to the toilets.

I locked the door and sat on the toilet. I opened the message from Number Withheld. It said, *I am watching you.*

I deleted the messages, I deleted all of them, even the ones I hadn't read. Then I wrapped up the phone in toilet paper and threw it into the bin. I didn't go back to the caravan, back to Ivan. I went to find Tilly instead.

I thought Tilly would want to ask me about the night surfing, but she was buzzing about Tank. I'd forgotten all about it. She was so excited, I didn't have the heart to tell her that I didn't feel like going.

'We *have* to dress up,' Tilly said. 'It'll be fun. Secret identities. You'd be a great catwoman.'

'Except I totally left my black PVC catsuit at home,' I said, deadpan.

Tilly looked at me with this strange expression. Then she said, 'Do you *really* own a PVC catsuit?'

I gave her a push. 'No! I can make jokes too, you know.'

'Hardy har har,' Tilly said. 'Ooh, I know! Let's go into Indigo and check out the op-shop.'

I shrugged. 'Okay. But I doubt the Indigo St Vinnie's has a PVC catsuit either.'

We walked up the road into town. Indigo has a pub, with heaps of pokies and a bistro, a few cafes (one great, the rest ordinary), two surf shops, a golf store, a fishing store, fish and chips, a huge newsagency — the shops you expect to see in a small town that's probably dead in winter and packed in summer. The op-shop is huge though, and really well laid out. Tilly's in love with it. Mieke too. She has an amazing eye for vintage clothes so she nearly always scores stuff that I would have thought were curtains or something. She can make anything work and she's really great with scissors and hand sewing. She'll buy some huge kaftan thing and the next day she's cut it and spent half the night sewing it and it's a really gorgeous dress that looks like it comes straight from a designer store.

I don't really do op-shops. I like shops where you get bags with the store's name printed on them. I like trying things on in spacious changerooms with lots of mirrors and people around to tell you if things work the way they're supposed to. I like — I know this is shallow — shops that make me feel rich, that only have one outfit in each size lined up neatly in a row, where things cost lots of money and not any old person can shop there. I'm not that into bargains. Don't get me wrong, I've been saving money since I started working at the Loveshack, but I'd rather buy one amazing piece of clothing every couple of months than buy stacks of cheap stuff. Mum buys me clothes anyway. She loves to take me shopping; she calls it being 'one of the girls'. She'll buy me anything I like. As long as it's pink.

Nah, not really, but she often tries to steer me in that direction, towards the mixy-matchy pink, girly stuff that she used to dress me in when I was six years old.

Anyway, we were at the op-shop when suddenly I had an idea. I don't know where it came from, or what made me say it, or why it excited me so much. It wasn't a normal idea. It wasn't the kind of idea I'd usually have.

'Listen, Tilly. It's secret identities, right? So why don't I go as you, and you go as me?' It all came out in a rush, I wasn't even sure that it made sense, but Tilly tilted her head.

'How would it work?' she asked. Typical Tilly. She always wanted to work out the rules of the game before we played.

'I'll pick an outfit for you. You pick an outfit for me. We'll dress each other the way *we* would dress. See what I mean?'

'Okay,' Tilly said, hesitantly.

'So . . .' I took Tilly over to the size 8s and 10s. 'If I were you, what would you wear?'

She flicked through the rack. She pulled out a shapeless, one-size-fits-all Indian cotton, long-sleeve black top.

'With jeans or baggy denim shorts,' she said, handing it over to me. 'And probably your Birkenstocks.' When I tried it on it hung loosely around me. It was all right, not showy and not at all flattering, but it was comfortable. I looked at myself in the mirror. If my friends could see me now! The thought gave me a little thrill, as if being ordinary could also be kind of daring.

'Perfect,' I said.

'Are you sure?' Tilly asked. 'You usually look, you know . . . prettier.'

'It's *perfect*,' I said again, firmly. 'Now. It's your turn.'

I went over to the 12s.

'I'm a size 14,' said Tilly.

'No you're not,' I said. I held up a stretchy top and looked at the label. It was Club Zone, a ravewear brand. It had a zip down the front, with a V neckline and it was really well made. It was only three dollars too — I suddenly understood the appeal of the Indigo op-shop. This was definitely something I would wear.

'Try it on,' I said.

Tilly stared at the top and then at me, like she was scared to touch it.

'Come on.' I thrust it at her.

She took it into the changeroom.

'Have you got it on?' I called out ages later. She'd gone all quiet and still.

'Yes,' she said, in this meek voice.

'Well? Show me.'

Tilly stepped out. She stood there with the fluorescent lights of the op-shop flickering on her, so her skin looked a bit purple and goosebumpy. She looked awkward, but actually the top looked great, it clung to her curves like a bathing suit, and the cut of the sleeves emphasised her strong arms.

'I can't wear this,' Tilly said.

'Why not?'

'*Because —*' she gestured wildly at her chest area. 'Boobs ahoy.'

The top was pretty low cut, and I suppose there was a bit of cleavage showing, but on Tilly it was really flattering. She must be, like a D. Maybe even a double D. And you know how girls with big boobs look a bit fat or weird-shaped if they wear a high-necked top? The V-neck was good for her. Trust me.

That's what I said to her. '*Trust* me. If you were me, I'd wear that. Come on, it's the rules.'

Tilly was a sucker for the rules. She turned around and looked in the mirror again. 'Okay,' she said, faintly. 'What should I wear it with?'

'Here, try these on.' I gave her some black hipsters. She sighed and took them in to try on. 'Yep,' I said when she came out. 'They'll do. Now. What about shoes?'

I haven't had so much fun shopping for clothes for like . . . ever. It was so much better picking stuff out for Tilly than for myself or my friends. I don't know why. Maybe it was because Tilly needed me, even if she didn't know it.

Our luck ran out when it came to shoes, and there was something about second-hand shoes that grossed me out anyway. In the end I said she could wear her black sandals but only if she painted her toenails. We went across the road to the chemist to get nail polish when I spied . . .

'One more thing,' I said, and I dragged Tilly over to the hairdresser.

'You want me to cut my hair?' said Tilly, stopping outside the door. We looked in. There was no one else in there, just a bored hairdresser flipping through a magazine.

'Short,' I said. She just *had* to. She couldn't stop now. I don't know why it mattered so much but it did. If she was going to be Zara for a night, I wanted her to cut her hair.

'But I —'

'You're me and it's my hair,' I said, bossily. I was already behaving more like Tilly. 'Short. Trust me, it will suit you.'

'How short?' Tilly said.

'*Short* short.'

She squeaked. 'I've never had short hair.'

'You always wear your hair up anyway. You may as well cut it off.' I was on a mission. 'Think how much cooler it will be for summer. It'll be fantastic. I promise.'

Tilly stood looking at me and suddenly I saw something in her face that reminded me of the night before, you know, like she *wanted* something. Really wanted it.

'Okay,' she said. 'Let's do it.'

I hovered over the hairdresser, giving instructions. '*Short* short. Like Judi Dench.'

'Judi Dench is old,' wailed Tilly.

Quickly, before Tilly could have second thoughts, I said, 'Judi Dench is classical, like you.' To the hairdresser I said. '*Classical* short. Isabella Rossellini. Um, Alyssa Milano in *Charmed*. Natalie Portman.'

'Natalie Portman! Didn't she shave her head?'

'After that, silly. Feminine. Razored.'

'Razored?' Tilly gulped.

'Textured,' I said quickly, before Tilly took off.

I expected the hairdresser to be a country hick, you know, all perms and mullets, but she wasn't at all. Her name was Saskia, and she had this accent, Dutch or something, and she totally knew what I meant. She cut Tilly's hair really short all over. Cut it away from her face, framing her, then finished off with this thing that was part blade and part comb to give it that razored look. It was tufty and kind of blunt, but soft. Strong, but not harsh. I felt this rush, like I was creating her. Was this how Mieke felt when she was making a painting appear on a blank page?

When Saskia was finished, Tilly paid in a daze.

'Do you have any product?' Saskia asked.

'Any what?' Tilly said.

'She doesn't,' I answered. I bought some for her (after all, I'd made her get her hair cut, it was the least I could do).

'Do you love it?' I asked Tilly when we left. I couldn't stop looking at her. 'Because I *love* it.'

'I guess,' said Tilly, touching her hair as if she couldn't quite believe it was gone.

'She did a brilliant job. Maybe I should get Saskia to cut mine too,' I said.

Tilly laughed. 'You can't.'

'Why not?'

'Because you're me,' Tilly pointed out. 'And I would *never* cut my hair.'

When we got back to the campground, I went to the toilets, fished through the bin (gross!) and found my phone. I unwrapped it. It was my phone, after all, I couldn't just chuck it away. There was only one new message. It was from Sooz. *Is everything ok? Why arent u answering ur messages?* I thumbed back: *everything's fine, reception is crap here* and sent it off. Just as I did, the phone started ringing. The call display lit up. I've got it programmed so it's green for friends, blue for family and red for everyone else. It was red. I looked at the incoming number, but all it said was 'number withheld'. I jabbed the answer button.

'Hello?'

But there was silence. I hung up. A few seconds later it rang again.

'Hello? Who is this?' They didn't reply. 'Just tell me who you are, you gutless creep . . .' But they'd already hung up.

The third time they called, I didn't answer the phone.

Chapter Ten
Tilly

Mum, Dad and Teddy had gone to Duncan River panning for gold, so I had time to get used to my new hair before I showed them. I kept sneaking into the shower block and peering at myself in the mirror. The mirror reflected back the drab concrete-brick interior of the shower block and there in the middle, shockingly, was me. I looked bright and extra real, television real — larger than life. Part of me felt exposed. Even though I wore my hair in a ponytail to combat scary frizz, there were always bits dangling in my face, over my ears. Now my ears were right there, my eyes too and my whole shiny forehead.

But I didn't hate it. I felt brave. My whole face was opened out. My eyes looked bigger and I don't know if

I was imagining it but my face looked fuller, less pointy. It seemed to flatten my cheekbones somehow. And it wasn't frizzy anymore, just kind of fuzzy and thatchlike, like a trimmed lawn. It's not as if I was an instant beauty but I was *interesting* to look at in a way I hadn't been before.

Zara helped me get ready for Tank. She put the product glop in my hair, and make-up on my face. I couldn't see what she was doing but it seemed there was an awful lot of gunk going on there. Though when I checked in the mirror the make-up was kind of subtle, much better than I would do. She'd used browny, bronzey colours, and though I still had freckles, the powder she'd put on last subdued them a bit.

I put on the outfit. Crikey. I felt like the Mistress of Doom in that top. Or the Borg Queen. But it also felt exciting. I was still a bit scared of my boobs. I kept tugging at the top until Zara slapped my hand away.

'The girls are on the loose,' I said in mock horror. Only I was genuinely horrified, so it was really mock-mock horror.

Zara snickered. 'Don't fiddle,' she instructed.

I think Dad, bless him, was a bit scared of my boobs too. My family had come home while we were getting changed, so there was a lot for them to take in all at once. I mean, when they left I had a ponytail, frizz, freckles *and* a uniform: baggy T-shirt, baggy shorts. When they came back I was a practically bald bondage mistress.

Teddy looked shy. Mum looked amazed. Dad looked . . . elsewhere.

'What are you going as?' Teddy asked.

The answer made *me* shy. 'Zara. And Zara's going as me.'

'You don't look anything like Zara! You still just look like Tilly but in someone else's clothes. Besides, why would Zara want to go as you?' Teddy asked. I swiped her. But I could see what she meant. I knew why I wanted to be Zara. Why wouldn't I? But why would Zara want to be me?

'Your beautiful hair,' Mum said a bit sadly.

'It wasn't beautiful,' I said. 'It was frizzy.'

'Mothers never want their daughters to cut their hair,' Mum said. 'It's a fact of life.' She tilted her head. 'You look so different. But it suits you. It's just a bit of a shock. Maybe *I* should . . .' Mum reached up to fiddle with her own hair. Suddenly everyone wants to cut their hair short? It was sort of flattering and annoying all at once.

I went into the tent to rummage around for my wallet and trade my thongs for sandals. Dad muttered something to Mum I couldn't quite hear, but it sounded like, 'Are you going to let her go out like that?' Apparently when it came to my boobs, Dad didn't want to be the boss.

Mum's voice rang out clearly. 'Clothes are a *perfectly safe* way for Tilly to experiment with her sexual identity, Jules. *I trust her completely.*' I am sure that was all for my benefit. It was Mum's way of saying that she wanted me to be careful. 'And besides,' she lowered her voice, 'remember what I was wearing on our first date?'

'Don't say *that*,' Dad groaned. 'Don't you remember where we —?'

'I can hear you!' I shouted through the tent wall. That shut them up.

The club was already pumping out the music when we arrived. Where had all these young people come from? I guess some were Indigo locals, some were tourists, and others probably came from neighbouring towns. I suppose not much happens if you're a teenager out this way and you're looking for a bit of doof or a chance to shake your booty.

Zara left me at the door. Only she wasn't Zara anymore, I was. The only trouble is, I had no idea how to be Zara. I'd only ever been Tilly. And maybe I wasn't even very good at that.

When it came to dancing, Zara had instructed, less is more. Move, but not too much. How much was too much? I stood in the middle of the room and swayed slightly, waiting for people to come to me because I'm Zara. I'm the kind of person people just want to be near, because I let off this golden glow of popularity. Yup.

Because I knew I was being Zara and not myself, I kept dancing, even though I felt glaringly alone and self-conscious. Zara had disappeared to hang out at the couches in the dark corner (which was where I wanted to be). It seemed Zara was better at being Tilly than I was at being Zara.

As people moved to make space for me on the dance floor, I fought my fight-or-flight instinct. Every part of me was screaming to run away. People were looking at me, and not because I was being funny, but because I was — shudder — dancing. I concentrated on the music. I told myself firmly that everyone's kind of alone on the dance floor, unless you're one of those couples that kiss and dance at the same time. Like the couple that kept bumping into me.

I swayed around the dance floor, moving, but not too much, but I managed to bump into someone anyway. I was pretty sure Zara didn't bump. She seemed to have an uncanny grasp of her personal space. I turned around, fighting the urge to apologise, because I thought if Zara did bump she was probably good at ever so slightly making it the other person's fault. Anyway, it was Ivan.

'Sorry,' he muttered to my boobs and continued to look around.

'Ivan! It's me, Tilly.'

He looked again. It gave me a swelling feeling in my stomach, the good kind, to think he hadn't recognised me. Did I really look *that* different? I felt different. I could feel all this air round my head and bare shoulders and my — ahem — cleavage.

Ivan frowned at me and for a moment I thought he still didn't know who I was. 'Is Zara here?'

I didn't tell him that was actually a trick question.

'She's around,' I said, shrugging. It was hard being cool because Ivan smelled really, really good and it was making me breathe in quick breaths. I could feel the pulse in my neck throbbing, and I wondered if he could see it.

'She was behaving strangely,' he said. 'She was kind of jumpy. And did you see what she was wearing?' His lip curled in vague disbelief and maybe a shade of horror. Or mock-mock horror.

'Yes,' I said, trying not to sound defensive. After all, Zara was me. So that was my outfit he was dissing. 'But it is a theme night. What are you here as?'

Ivan blinked.

'You could be Peter Parker,' I said. 'You can't be Clark Kent because he wore glasses. But Peter Parker didn't really have a disguise, he just looked sort of soft and gormless.' Ivan raised his eyebrows. Had I just called him soft and gormless? 'Or . . . I know! You could be, like, on *Star Trek* when they land on Earth in the past, only it's like our present, and have to pretend to be one of the locals and try and fit in with the latest fashions.' Suddenly I realised I was being too Tilly, I was a twittering fool. Ivan continued to stare at me. The more he stared, the more I wanted to talk. So I looked away, channelled my inner-Zara, shrugged and said, in an I-don't-really-care-about-anything voice (you know, that voice that girls use that's a bit like a cat yawning), 'Or, you know. Like, whatever.'

It wasn't just about being Zara. His expressionless face was starting to irritate me. He offered nothing. He was kind of hard work.

'You cut your hair,' he said finally. I was torn between being annoyed that it took him so long to notice and being all melty and puddle-like because he *had* noticed.

How does Zara do it? I mean she has boyfriends, right? How does she stay so cool around them? I should ask him to dance, I thought. Would Zara do that? Or would she just beguile them into asking her? Considering I was only Zara for one night, I didn't think it was realistic to expect beguilement. I opened my mouth to ask Ivan. But the words didn't come. I was just standing there with my mouth open. Stuff like this would never happen to Zara.

Ivan stood looking at me for like five whole seconds (which doesn't seem like a long time when you write it down, but it is when it's Ivan Sutherland looking at you), then suddenly he looked away. 'Well. Have a good time, Tilly,' he said curtly and he walked off. Leaving me bamboozled, I can tell you. I was relieved to see him go. I couldn't be Zara around Ivan, I just wasn't cool enough for that. Besides, he was kind of my brother tonight and that was just icky.

But even after he left, I could still smell his aftershave, as if it was hovering, a perfect Ivan-shaped cloud of phero-mones, exactly where Ivan had been standing.

I dithered, which is almost the same as dancing, but with less swaying. Part of me was willing to give it another shot. I had the outfit. I had the haircut. I had the make-up, the mask. Part of me really wanted this to work. But another part of me screamed to go and find Zara and beg her to trade back. Was I really willing to admit failure so soon?

'Tilly? You came!'

I turned around. It was Sawyer. He looked amazing. He was wearing a tux, which really set off his dark-lashed eyes.

Remember I said he was indie rock hot? Well, that night he was a runaway smash hit.

'Bond?' I guessed.

'James Bond,' he replied, very seriously, with a Sean Connery accent.

'Does that *really* count as a secret identity?' I asked. 'James Bond is the most famous superspy ever.'

He looked me up and down, 'I don't think I *want* to know what you are. Wait. Yes, I do. I really do.'

'Well,' I said, coyly. 'It's supposed to be secret identities.'

'Not telling, huh?' Sawyer asked, with his lazy grin. 'Wanna be a Bond girl?'

Call me slow, but it was only at that moment I realised we were dancing. I mean, I was dancing and he was dancing and he was leaning over to talk right into my ear, occasionally cupping my arm with his hand . . . so, we were dancing together. Now, that's a big deal. It's never happened to me before. I've danced *near* boys. But usually when I dance I do it in a group, in a big circle, and sometimes there are incidental boys in the circle but mostly I'm with the other geeky girls. And, hello? He was touching me. He hadn't said anything for ages but his hand was still on my arm. He was smiling right at me, looking as if I was the only girl in the room. My skin under his hand felt like there were bugs crawling all over it, but in a good way. I was shy, painfully shy, but being Zara helped. I kept dancing.

'I take it back,' he said suddenly.

'What?' I asked.

'I take it back,' he said again, louder.

'No, I mean what do you take back?'

'I don't know *any* girls who look like you.'

And that was when I melted into a soft goop all over the floor.

Nah, not really. We just kept dancing.

Chapter Eleven

Zara

Sitting still was almost painful. The pounding repetitive bass was revving me up, I wanted to dance, to feel the music vibrate through me as if it was driving my body, stronger than blood, stronger than my own heart, beating against that big hard bone that sits in the middle of your chest.

When I go out – to clubs or raves or parties or whatever – there are always people who sit around the edge of the room, not dancing or anything, just talking or watching. I don't get it. How can they keep still? How can they not move? I'm like a puppet on strings once the music gets inside me. It's not about choice. You become part of something bigger, this throng of people, all driven by the same beat, as if you all have the same blood, the same heart. You're not you anymore, you're just part of the music, part of the place.

It's kind of like surfing, I guess. Except the sea's a dance-floor that dances back.

'No dancing,' Tilly had instructed. 'Sit. At the back.'

'But what do you *do*?'

Tilly shrugged. 'People-watch. Talk to other non-dancing geeks like me. Eat. Stay at home with my mum and dad and do the crossword. I don't really go out that much. Not to places like this.' She looked defensive. 'We don't have to do this, you know.'

I was quick to answer. 'I want to.' I couldn't explain my desperate desire to be Tilly for a night, or at least to not be Zara. Not to Tilly, not even to myself.

So I found somewhere to sit, up the back, away from the temptation of the dancefloor. There was a row of seats near the window where guests could sit and look out at the surf, lit up by the golf club floodlights. The building was set up high in the sand dunes, back from the beach, the golf greens spread out among the dunes. I watched the waves roll in. I felt this urge to be out there. I don't know how long I watched them for, but it was soothing, the beat of the music, the rise and fall of the waves, as if they were in tune with each other. After a while I didn't feel alone anymore. The club was disappearing, the waves seemed more real than anything else.

'Zara. *Zara.*'

Ivan sat down next to me. I don't know how many times he'd said my name. I leaned back in the chair and crossed my arms. 'What are you doing here?' I asked. Ivan never goes out. I mean he goes out, like, he leaves the house and stuff. But he doesn't go *out*. I stared at him, and said, suddenly suspicious, 'Are you checking up on me?'

Since when had Ivan cared what I was doing? He's been shrugging me off since I was three years old. By the time I was ten (I'm a slow learner) I didn't bother to follow him around anymore, I knew enough to know he'd never have time for his little sister. We weren't close, we were never close. I had more history with Tilly or Mieke than I did with Ivan.

'I didn't want another night with Mum and Dad in the caravan,' Ivan said. 'I thought I'd see what was happening here. Not really my scene, though.'

'Why don't you leave then?' I was being a bitch, but I couldn't work out what he was really doing there. I had an uncomfortable feeling that he knew about the text messages. What if he told Mum or, worse, Dad? I didn't want anyone to know about them. It was bad enough I had to read them. But to think of Dad reading those things — *Zara Sutherland is a pricktease* — made me shudder. And, like I said, since when did Ivan care?

Ivan looked at me with this wounded-dog look.

'See ya, Zara,' he said. And he did leave. I remembered I was supposed to be Tilly. I felt bad. She wouldn't have treated Ivan like that, especially not her own brother. But before I could follow him, some other guy sat down where Ivan had been.

'Pretty amazing view,' he said, leaning in towards me and raising his voice over the music.

I was about to shrug. I felt my face close over, that seal of boredom taking over my features. But I was Tilly. Suddenly I was furious with Ivan, it was his fault. He'd made me be Zara again.

Tilly talked to anyone and everyone, young and old, ugly or not. Not that this guy was ugly. He was all right, just ordinary looking.

'Yeah, it is,' I said. 'Amazing.'

'Not dancing?' he asked.

'I'm not much of a dancer.'

'Me either. Is that a costume?'

I looked down at myself. 'Kind of,' I said. 'What about you?' I nodded at his clothes, an ordinary shirt and jeans.

'I'm in the witness protection program,' he said.

Okay, it was kind of clever. I know Tilly would appreciate it, so I laughed politely.

'Do you want a drink?' he asked, raising his own glass as if to demonstrate what a drink was.

I shook my head. Tilly was way too sensible to let a strange guy buy her drinks.

'If you don't dance and you don't drink, what do you do?'

'I don't really know,' I said. I looked around, hoping to find someone else to talk to. There was something about this guy that made me uncomfortable. Where were the groups of geeks that Tilly said she talked to? There were a few groups but I felt funny about inserting myself into one of them. It's not like I have trouble making friends, but usually I don't think about it. Somehow being Tilly was making me self-conscious.

It was then that I noticed Tilly was leaving. She was heading off the dancefloor, and I hoped for a moment she was coming this way. But she wasn't alone. She was with a guy. It took me a moment to recognise it was Sawyer, the waiter, looking all studly in a tux. He had his hand on her back and was steering her protectively through the crowd and out the door onto the deck. Tilly was in a daze.

Suddenly it was me that was feeling protective. Tilly wasn't used to guys like Sawyer. What if, when she was pretending to be me, she ended up doing something she might regret later? But I couldn't just barge out there and demand to know what he was up to. I didn't want to embarrass her. Then I remembered I was Tilly. Would Tilly come looking for me? I thought about the night before, how she was waiting for me when I came out of the surf.

Witness Protection guy was saying something to me.

'What?'

'I said it's loud in here. The music.'

'Yeah, it is,' I said. 'I'm going outside.'

He followed me. It wasn't till he started walking that I realised he was drunk. He was mostly fine but he stumbled out the door onto the deck. There were a few couples out there and a group of girls, but I couldn't see Tilly and Sawyer.

'What's your name, anyway?' he asked.

I hesitated. 'Matilda,' I said.

'Waltzing Matilda,' he said.

'Yeah, like I've never heard that one before.' I knew Tilly got it all the time. 'Look, I'll see you later. I've got to find my friend.'

'Okay,' he said. But he didn't leave.

I walked to the edge of the deck and looked out. The path was lit intermittently between the club and the beach but I couldn't see them.

There were two directions they could have gone. One was down the path towards the beach, which would be bad because there were lots of little paths that came off the main path into the dunes and then of course the beach itself was huge, so the chances of finding them were slim. The other direction was back around the clubhouse to the resort, where the main courtyard and the pool were. Witness Protection followed me down the steps. I decided to try the courtyard first.

To be honest I didn't know *who* I was now, Tilly or Zara, but I guess I had enough of Tilly left in me not to tell Witness Protection to piss off. Besides, he was kind of droopy and harmless looking, a bit bleary from alcohol and just sort of . . . well, like I said, ordinary.

'Where are we going?' he asked a couple of times, blinking.

'I just want to find my friend,' I answered.

'What's she look like?'

'Um, she's got short hair. She's wearing a black top. She's with a guy called Sawyer.'

'Sawyer,' Witness Protection said knowingly. 'Eye for the lay-deez.' He sounded like a bad drivetime radio DJ.

'Yeah, that Sawyer.'

Witness Protection spoke very earnestly, the way people do when they're drunk and they really want to get a point across. 'Look, Sawyer's a good bloke. Trust him with my life. 'S a top bloke.' Then he made some vaguely rude gesture and said again, 'Eye for the *lay*-deez.' I quickened my pace, hoping to leave him behind.

I got to the courtyard. Damn. They weren't there. Which meant the beach path. I turned around. Witness Protection was standing at the entrance of the path, swaying slightly. He'd pulled a small bottle of something out of a pocket, it looked like whisky or brandy, something brown and nasty.

'Drink?' he asked.

'No, thank you,' I said, stepping to one side to get past him. But he sidestepped too and blocked my way.

'Come on,' he leered. 'Put hairs on your chest.'

'Listen, I just want to find my friend. Do you mind getting out of my way?'

'How about a kiss first? Come on, just a kiss.' He leaned forward.

I tried to push past. He grabbed my arm.

'I'm *not* kissing you,' I said, pulling my arm free.

'Then I'm not letting you pass,' he said. He was still drunk, but something, adrenaline maybe, or expectation, made him stand up straighter. His eyes were bright, his voice was clearer.

Call me slow, but that was when I realised how stupid I was, coming up a dimly lit path on my own with a drunk guy I didn't even know. I'd felt protected, being Tilly. I'd felt safe, shielded by my dowdy costume, by my new identity. But I was still Zara. I was still this girl. Words crawled under my skin: *pricktease, you want this, I'm watching you.*

I shoved Witness Protection guy, hard enough that he lost his footing and stumbled back into the spiky grass growing on the sandy mound behind him. I gave him a hard kick for good measure then I ran down the path. My breath was in my ears and my jaw was set so hard it hurt. My vision was jerking around because I was running and my eyes hadn't adjusted yet, but I wasn't scared. I wasn't anything. I wasn't Tilly. I was never really Tilly. I was nothing, I felt nothing. A tightness in my chest and a cramping muscle in my leg, that's all. That was all I was.

Memories flashed – I'd felt exactly like this the night of Kayla's party. After I walked in on Marcus and Kayla, I'd run down the stairs and out the front door. I'd forgotten Tang Yi. I was desperate to leave. I saw Rio getting in the car with these two guys – Dante, her boyfriend, and Dante's brother. I couldn't remember his name then, but I know now: Lochie. He was blond, his hair stuck straight up and he had a square forehead and the bridge of his nose was really long. Actually I could picture his face right then better than Witness Protection's, better even than Marcus's.

'Are you going now?' I'd asked Lochie as he opened the driver's door. 'Right now?'

Lochie shrugged. 'Yeah, I guess. Wanna ride?'

I looked at Lochie's car, an old Toyota. Dad always said Toyotas were reliable, right?

Later I told myself I didn't know for sure that he'd been drinking . . . but it was a lie. His eyes were bright and he was slurring his words. Rio and Dante certainly had been. As soon as they got into the back seat they started kissing; I could hear Rio moaning as I slid in the seat beside Lochie and did up my seatbelt.

Lochie paid no attention to them, or to me either. He revved the engine and pulled sharply away from the kerb.

'Hey, watch it,' Dante said. Rio giggled. I looked out the window. As Lochie veered violently to one side, then wrested the car back into his control, I felt nothing. I was thinking about nothing.

Out of the corner of my eye, in the shadows of the dunes just off the path, I saw Tilly and Sawyer. I stopped running. Tilly had her arms crossed over her body, she was looking down at her feet. Sawyer was walking behind her, his arms down by his side. They were walking back towards the golf club.

'Tilly!' I called. She looked up.

'Zara, are you leaving? Have you been running? What's going on?'

'I just met a really *nice* friend of yours,' I said savagely to Sawyer.

'Who?'

I looked up the path. Witness Protection guy was on the stairs on his way back to the golf club.

'Him.' I pointed.

Sawyer looked. 'Bundy? He's no friend of mine.'

'That's not what he said. Reckons you're a real *top bloke*.'

Tilly looked at Sawyer, confused, before asking me gently, 'Did he hurt you?'

I said, 'He was piss-weak.' My voice was cold, it was harsh, like splinters.

'Do you want me to walk you girls back to the campsite?' Sawyer asked.

'No,' said Tilly, quickly. 'We'll be fine. Won't we, Zara?' She reached out and clasped my hand tightly.

'Yes,' I said, looking down numbly at her hand in mine. It should feel warm, I thought. But it didn't. It felt cool. Maybe it was me. Maybe I wasn't feeling things the way I was supposed to.

I couldn't work out what had happened between Sawyer and Tilly. Had he tried it on with her too? Was this a town of drunks and date-rapists? Is that what they considered romance around here?

'Come on,' Sawyer said to Tilly. 'Just let me walk you some of the way. I only want to . . .'

'You heard her, Cowboy,' I snapped. I just wanted him to go away. 'I hear you've got a real eye for the ladies. Well, there's plenty more inside. I'm sure you can find someone just your type.'

Tilly flinched. She wouldn't look at Sawyer. But she let go of my hand.

'You don't know anything about me,' he said coolly, but I had a feeling he was actually talking to Tilly. 'Good night, Tilly.'

'See you,' she said, without feeling. As he walked up the path she called after him, 'And hey, tell your mate Bundy, Zara's dad is a cop.'

'I already told you,' Sawyer called back, 'he's not my mate.'

'Well,' I muttered, 'he's certainly not mine.'

Chapter Twelve
Tilly

Okay, I admit it. I felt terrible as I watched Sawyer walk away.

On the dancefloor, Sawyer leaned in close and hollered over the pumping music, 'It's getting pretty loud in here. Want to go for a walk?'

I nodded, dazed. First he'd wanted to dance and now this? He steered me towards the door, his hand on my arm. No boy had ever guided me like that. It made me feel two things: like I was kind of enclosed, his body curving around my body – it was nice. But it also made me feel like I was giving myself over to him too easily, giving up my self-control. I was so confused. I wanted to melt into him, to be Princess to his Charming, but it went against everything

I believed in about women being strong, not giving up all their power to the first sexy guy who comes along.

Out on the deck he said, 'Shall we go somewhere more private?'

I looked out at the sea, and remembered Zara the night before, her pale form, surfing ghost-waves. Suddenly I wanted to be out there, I wanted to be a ghost, to give up being a human girl. I wanted to run from Sawyer and hide in the ocean. The cold air reminded me how much of me was exposed. I shivered as I felt it prickle my shoulders and chest, like fingertips, like the lightest, faintest touch. But then I looked at Sawyer. And I knew I wanted him. I wanted to be here beside him, I wanted to be touched. It was making me dizzy, veering so wildly from one complete set of feelings to another entirely contradictory set.

We went down the path, off into the shadowy dunes. We sat on the edge of the velvety green of the golf course. I took off my shoes and curled my toes into the soft grass. I had nothing to say to him. Words dried up in my throat. I was acutely aware of him beside me, sitting close enough that I could feel heat coming off him, although we weren't quite touching. I don't know how long we sat like that, not talking. Probably only a minute or two, but it felt like eons passed, like whole civilisations could have risen out of the dunes and collapsed back into the sand in that time. I guess part of me was still being Zara – cool and aloof. But my body was far from aloof. I wanted to feel his hands on me, but I didn't know how to cross the space between us and make it happen. I could feel an energy coming off him. I knew he wanted to touch me. So why wasn't he?

'You're quiet tonight,' he said. 'You seem . . . different.'

Different from what? But I nodded, not looking at him. He was right. Everything about me was different. Being shy — painfully, mutely shy — was a new feeling for me. I actually felt physical discomfort, my inner cheeks felt raw and swollen, and I had to keep swallowing down excess saliva. Occasionally I had this lurching sensation in my stomach, like going down in a lift.

'Are you cold?'

I shook my head.

He edged closer. He looked at me curiously, as if he genuinely wasn't sure what I was thinking.

'Shall we warm up with . . .' He leaned closer. I closed my eyes. This was it. I couldn't breathe. I felt the warmth of his breath when he finished with, 'a game of golf?'

My eyelids sprung open. 'What?'

'She speaks! Come on.' He leapt up. 'I'll tee off.' He swiped at the air with an imaginary golf club. 'Fore!' he called.

'I don't know how to play,' I said.

'You've been coming to the golf club all these years and you've never played a game of golf before? Stand up.' I stood up. 'Now, since you're a beginner I suggest a nine iron for you.'

His miming was quite convincing. I almost forgot that there was no actual nine iron, and that it was the middle of the night and that I was alone with Sawyer. I took the nine iron and tentatively tried a practice swing. It was kind of fun. The tension eased a bit; I stopped feeling so vulnerable. I placed my invisible ball on an imaginary tee and swung my club up high.

'What are you trying to do, chop wood?' said Sawyer.

'Excuse me!' I put a hand on one hip. ' It *is* my first time. Bit of space, if you don't mind.'

'Here. Let me show you.'

Sawyer stepped up behind me. I inhaled and forgot to exhale as he wrapped his arms around me, putting his hands on my hands.

'Now, swing it up, and follow through with your body. It's not from your wrists or your elbow, it comes from here . . .' he put his hands on my diaphragm, a strong, firm pressure. Man's hands. 'Try again,' he said in my ear. I raised my arms and strangely I could feel what he meant about a golf swing coming from the torso rather than the arms. 'That's better. And follow through.'

'I bet you say that to all the girls,' I said.

Sawyer's voice raised tiny hairs in my ear. 'Only this one,' he said. 'I've never played pretend golf at midnight before.'

My guard was well and truly down. I turned my face to look up at his. He still had his arms around me. Our noses were almost touching, I realised he was closing in. He bit his lip gently. I looked at his perfect teeth and imagined him biting *my* lip like that.

I pressed myself against him, raising my mouth towards his. It was my first kiss, but I bet it wasn't Zara's first kiss. Or Sawyer's either. It was clumsy at first and I started to pull back, embarrassed. But Sawyer put his hand on the back of my head and kissed me again. I did feel his tooth gently press down on my lower lip, which sent a rush of what felt like pure bliss travel right down from my lip to the tips of my naked toes.

But it wasn't my lip he was biting, was it? Tonight, it was Zara's. It was Zara he was out here with. Zara in the revealing tight black top, who cuts her hair fashionably short, who dances alone, and goes outside with boys onto deserted golf greens. But Zara was experienced, she knew what she was doing. Tilly knew nothing about this at all. Who was I kidding? I didn't have what it took to be Zara.

I pushed him away and stepped back. 'What?' he said. 'What's wrong?'

'Nothing. I have to go.'

'Are you kidding?'

'I'm sorry. I'm not . . . this isn't me. I don't do this.' I was babbling, backing away from him, looking for my shoes. He stood there watching me, looking half amused and half annoyed. He seemed so sure of himself. I envied him.

'What isn't you?'

'*This*. Any of this.' I gestured wildly towards myself. Suddenly I thought I might *cry*. No, please no. Where were my freaking shoes?

'Tilly, what's going on?'

'Nothing. I have to . . .' I stood on my sandal. I tried to jam my foot into it without undoing the buckle but I couldn't, so I sat down on the grass, feeling like a little kid as I pushed the thick leather strap through the buckle and fumbled around trying to get the pin through the hole.

'I didn't mean to rush you,' Sawyer said. 'You seemed so different tonight, the way you're dressed, the way you . . . I thought you *wanted* to kiss me.'

Well, of course I wanted to. I wanted to kiss him and more. I wanted to throw myself *into* him, to lose myself completely. I wanted to so badly it scared me. It scared me to think how far, how fast I wanted to go. This wasn't me. I didn't even *know* who I was anymore.

But I'm not stupid. For the first time in my life, a guy gets me alone on a deserted golf course in the middle of the night, teaches me how to play imaginary golf and then tries to kiss me . . . Of course I know what he wanted. He wanted Zara. Even if that night *I* was Zara, that was the girl he wanted — with the hair and the boobs and the dancing and the non-verbal. He didn't want Tilly. He didn't even *know* Tilly.

Sawyer followed me out of the dunes. I couldn't tell if he was disappointed or pissed off. I was so relieved to see Zara. At least it meant I didn't have to deal with my feelings. Or his.

'Are you sure you're okay?' I asked Zara. 'What were you doing out here with him anyway?'

'Don't worry about me. I'm fine. I can handle myself.'

I didn't doubt it. 'I was more worried about you, going off with Sawyer.'

'You don't trust him either, huh?' I said wryly.

Zara looked at me apologetically. 'Men are scum?' she offered.

'Actually, he was really nice. He was *really* nice,' I admitted. 'But this isn't me. It's just an outfit and a hair-cut. And, you know.' I adjusted my top. 'Two really scary boobs.'

'I don't think he thought they were scary,' Zara said. 'I think he probably thought *they* were nice.'

'Yeah, but that's the problem, isn't it? I mean, I hardly said anything tonight. He knows nothing about me, besides what my boobs look like. Frankly,' I tugged at my top. 'I'm kind of looking forward to putting them away again.'

'For what it's worth, Till, you really do look beautiful tonight.' Zara's voice softened. 'Maybe he just really likes you.'

I shrugged. 'Maybe. So . . .' I looked at Zara. 'Not an unmitigated success then.'

'What?'

'The whole identity swap thing. I mean, I don't know about you, but I had a massive existential crisis.'

'Yeah,' said Zara. 'Except I don't know what that means. But I think I did too.'

'It wasn't all bad, being you. I liked the dancing. I liked the boys. But –'

'Boy-s?' said Zara. 'More than one?'

'Oh well . . .' I'd been thinking of Ivan. 'No. Um, boy. I liked the boy. I liked the *idea* of the boy.'

'I didn't like the boy,' said Zara. 'But I didn't hate being Tilly.'

'That's kind of you to say. But I think when it comes down to it, I'm just not very good at being you,' I said. 'I mean, I'm still me. I just don't think a Tilly can be a Zara. Or a Zara can be a Tilly.'

'Me either,' said Zara, but she sounded even more regretful than I did. I glanced sideways at her closed face and wondered again why on earth Zara would want to be me.

We walked out of the dunes and onto the open beach. We both stopped and looked at the lit-up waves. I felt a desperate longing to be out there, to swim towards the inky line of the horizon.

'You still up for it?' Zara asked.

I nodded. I couldn't speak. No words could express how up for it I was, without me sounding like . . . like Tilly, and even though being Zara hadn't been as successful as I'd hoped, I realised I wasn't ready to go back to being Tilly. Not yet.

I was almost sick with excitement and nervousness as, silently, we entered the water, pushing our surfboards ahead of us, hearing the water gently slosh over the fibreglass boards. The golf club floodlights lit up the surface of the water; even so, visibility was minimal. I couldn't see below the dark surface. I couldn't see the horizon. There was a waxing half moon in the sky, but clouds drifted over it; it was faint and far away. There were stars too. That was one of the things I loved about Indigo. Living in inner city Melbourne, it was never really dark. All the light from the city meant the sky stayed a faint grey-blue colour, and the stars scattered across the sky were diminished by house and streetlights. But in Indigo, the stars crowded in, close together, as though they were peering at you in little gossipy conversational clusters. You could even see the Milky Way, white painterly streaks in the sky, like cappuccino froth smeared on a table.

I felt as if I was paddling out towards the stars, as if it was the night sky I was heading for. Ivan's board felt big and boatish underneath me and there was too much sway behind me, like being in the back seat of a station wagon. My own board was back at the campground, still strapped to the roof of our car. Zara had offered me hers, but I felt like I was intruding as it was. When we couldn't find a second legrope, I'd bravely volunteered to go without. As far as bravado went, it was pretty much false, but now, heading out towards the inky night sky, I had a sudden flash of feeling free. I felt like the real thing. It wasn't a comfortable feeling, in fact my stomach was churning more than the waves. It wasn't a familiar feeling either. Was *this* what it was like to be Zara, free-falling through life, no safety net in sight?

We got out beyond the break and straddled our boards, looking out towards the invisible horizon, waiting for a wave. I was panting, breathing the salty air deep into my lungs. Zara was quiet. I could make her out, the shape of her, though I couldn't see her face. Suddenly I knew I was intruding. Of course Zara didn't want me here. I'd pushed in to something private, stomped around on it with typical Tilly indelicacy.

I shivered and rubbed my arms. My legs dangling in the water were all right, but out of the water it was cold. I was ready to get moving. Silently and obligingly a wave began to form under me. I lay down on my board and turned into it, paddling my guts out.

'Tilly,' Zara called. 'Close your eyes!'

But it was too late, the floodlights had blinded me. Droplets of light scattered all around me. I closed my eyes to get rid of the glare. I should have pulled out of the wave but I kept going. I knew I was disoriented, but I thought if I stood up, the board would lead me where I needed to go. Of course it didn't. Surfboards aren't that tame. It bucked me off like a wild horse and I went in. The water slammed against me like a cold, hard, shattering mirror and I lost my breath for a moment. I hit the sandy bottom, landing on the soft part of my arm. I drifted underneath, dazed, waiting for my ankle cord to snap tight, but then I remembered, I wasn't attached to the board. I swam up quickly, panicking, my heart stuttering, my lungs bursting. Clawing blindly, my hands struck Ivan's board. I grabbed it before I lost it to the waves, hanging on as I spat out saltwater, coughing it out of my lungs.

Zara called out, 'Hey, Tilly, are you okay?'

I gasped. 'I'm fine. Really.' I laughed, weakly. I hauled myself back on the board.

'You sure.'

'Yeah!' I said. 'Bring it on.' Could Zara tell I was faking? The truth was I was losing heart. I was wet and cold, it was dark, and I was spooked. But I couldn't admit it to Zara. Besides, I'd come out here for a reason. I'd been looking for something. Would I forgive myself if I just gave up? I'd already done that once tonight, with Sawyer. I sat on the board nervously, watching the waves roll in.

The waves weren't huge, but to me, in the darkness, they felt like the fifty-year storm in *Point Break*. I listened to Zara as she told me how to feel my way, not relying on my sight. And I tried. I really did. I wanted to trust that my body would know what to do, that my other heightened senses would guide me. But as I attempted to mount each wave, I couldn't help but squint into the brightness. I pulled out of every wave at the last minute.

I decided to go back in, admit defeat. Let's face it, I totally sucked. I felt heavy and cumbersome, trapped in the uselessness of my body. I couldn't let myself go, I couldn't match the rhythm of the waves with my body. I had no instincts, no intuition. I was trying to use my brain, but out here my brain made me clumsy. I was no Zara.

I called out to Zara that I was going in. But just as I struck out towards the shore, I felt a wave building beneath me and the board lifted out of the water. What the hell,

I thought. One last time. As I paddled furiously to the top of the wave I closed my eyes tight. I stood up and found my balance. I opened my eyes. I was skimming along the water, parallel to the shore, and though the lights were shining straight at me, I didn't look at them, I looked down at the board slicing through the wave. I got it. Suddenly, for this brief, illuminating flash, I understood everything, how the whole world connected up. I saw with Zara's eyes. It was like, for one moment, I was truly inside her skin. The tempo of the waves passed up from the sea and into me, as if I was conducting the sea's energy, a powerful force rushing through me. It made me think of Sawyer's tooth on my lip, Sawyer's salty kiss.

I shouted out, with a burst of euphoria. I glanced back to see Zara, the ghost of her, this pale figure in the golf club lights, skimming the surface of the same wave. Maybe it was my imagination, surely it was too dim to see, but I could have sworn a huge grin was on her face. I spun back around.

That's when it all went horribly, horribly wrong. Maybe I slipped a bit or lost my balance, maybe my weight distribution changed. All I knew was that the board flipped up, right into the air, and spun me around. There was a moment where I swear I saw the board hovering in the sky and I thought it was going to crash down on me. My eyes had a moment to look at that board in the sky and then I was down, under the black water. It burned my throat and my lungs. I plummeted like a stone, down, down to the sand. I cracked my head on a rock; I felt it tear into the skin of my scalp. I tried to swim up, but my head was thudding. I think I might even have lost consciousness for a second. My chest was tighter than a drum and I kept wanting to breathe except some glimmering instinct told me I was still underwater and breathing was a really, *really* bad idea.

Finally I managed to push myself upwards. I broke up through the water's surface and tore my lungs apart with oxygen. The lights from the golf club shone blinding white, searing my retinas. I searched the water with my hands, looking for my board, but it was gone. The water swallowed me again. Sobbing, I pushed myself back up out of the water.

And this time when I surfaced everything went utterly, terrifyingly black.

Chapter Thirteen

Zara

Having Tilly out there with me, for some reason, made me feel lonely, like how the stars in the sky look close but really they're all millions of miles apart, each of them drifting in empty skies.

At first I hadn't wanted Tilly to come. But as we'd paddled side by side through the water, I'd started to feel the same excited anticipation as last time, and having Tilly beside me seemed to enhance it rather than detract from it.

But I could see that she didn't get it. Tilly was being pounded by every wave, and the longer we stayed out there, the harder she took it. She was tense, fighting the waves. She was trying to be the boss of the sea. I tried to explain about surfing by feel, to describe how I did it, but she just seemed to get more frustrated.

'I *need* my eyes,' she argued. 'I can't just do it by feel. My body doesn't get what to do.'

I was relieved when she said she was going back in. I watched her paddle away. The waves were building. It wasn't till I was standing that I realised Tilly had chosen to surf one more wave. It was a good wave, she was steady on her feet. I was elated on her behalf. I laughed as I surfed behind her. I knew what she was feeling 'cause I felt it too. We were both there, at the same time. Zara and Tilly, Tilly and Zara. It didn't matter anymore; we were the same.

I don't know what happened. Suddenly the big white board flipped up into the air, reflecting the golf club lights, doing one spin in the air before dropping back down.

'Tilly!' I dived into the water. I swam up and got my bearings, swimming out as hard as I could with the board beneath me, searching for Tilly and her board. But I couldn't see any sign of her.

I cupped my hands around my mouth and called out to her.

'Tilly! Til-ly!'

I'd done surf rescue at school, but this was different. This was real. There wasn't someone just bobbing around neatly in the water with their arm straight up like they knew the answer in a maths class. Where was she? Had she hit her head, or was she caught under the water somewhere,

113

her arm or leg trapped between rocks or tangled in seaweed? Was there a shark? Where exactly had she gone down? Was she actually metres away, in any direction? Would I be able to find her?

'Tilly!' I called. Shit. Shit. Should I dive in? Should I detach myself from the board and search for her under the water? No, that was crazy, I'd just exhaust myself. I sat up on my board, looking around wildly, thinking every lump, every wave, every sparkle of foam was her. I couldn't act. I just didn't know what to do.

And then the lights went out.

I cannot tell you how dark it was when that happened. It wasn't just like night dark. It was like the world had ended. It was like when the lights went out, everything had gone. Tilly, her surfboard, the golf club, everything in the world, vanished. Suddenly I knew I had to go in and get help. If I kept paddling around searching for her in the pitch black I'd exhaust myself, get disoriented, get lost as well and then I would never be able to save her.

I paddled towards the shore, turned my back on the sea. I hated doing that. Like I was turning my back on Tilly. I knew it was the right thing to do, but another part of me felt like I was giving up on her.

Suddenly, in my mind, I saw Rio in the back seat of the car, Dante outside the car, Lochie dragging him away. 'We've gotta go. Come on, man. We've gotta *go*.' Dante pulled away from Lochie. When I think about all this, I don't know where I am. I can't see me, but I was there. I know I was there. The back doors were crumpled in. Both of them were jammed. Dante must have climbed over the front seats to get out.

I dumped my board, clawing off my ankle strap — why hadn't I insisted Tilly wear one? Why hadn't I given her my board and I could have taken Ivan's, since I'd had more practice? I was about to take off up the beach when suddenly it occurred to me to dig my lurid pink surfboard into the sand over the tideline so we would know where to look for her. I did it as quickly as I could, though fear made me clumsy. Leaving the surfboard behind, leaving Tilly was hard. It was so hard.

Dante rang the ambulance. Why did it take so long to come? And then the police came. Lochie was furious, he was kicking the car while they tried to get Rio out, swearing at the ambos, trying to pick a fight with one of the cops, but it was Dante he was really furious with, Dante who'd betrayed him, going back for Rio. It was so ugly. So blunt and awful. And Rio, I couldn't tell then that she was okay. Where was I? They'd both forgotten about me, Dante and Lochie.

Then my dad showed up.

I ran up the beach, past the beach boxes, up towards the campsite. Running again, always running, running away from, running towards. Running just to run. Running to go faster. Running like a kid, running with the wind inside me. Everything so dark, jumping at shadows, like there was somebody there, waiting for me, waiting to get me alone, stepping out of the shadows. *Pricktease. You know you want it.* No. Run faster. Run for Tilly.

I missed the path to the campsite twice. There were no lights now, except for the feeble streetlight above the beach box, nothing to guide me. I was crying by the time I found it, stumbling back and forth on the beach, searching with my eyes and my hands in the beachy scrub and ti-trees for the narrow path.

The campsite, at least, was lit, the toilet blocks and the occasional street light making Mum and Dad's caravan easy to find. I went to the annexe and woke Ivan. He rubbed his face and blinked his eyes open.

'Zara? What? What is it?' he mumbled.

'It's Tilly,' I said. 'She's missing.'

'Missing?' He wasn't sitting up. I shook him. I knew he was only half awake.

'I can't find her. Ivan, you have to come back to the beach with me. We need to go now.'

'The beach?' He sat up. 'You're wet! Have you been swimming? What time is it?'

I was pulling at him, half dragging him out of bed. 'We have to go now. They turned off the lights. Please, Ivan —'

'Zara, you have to calm down and tell me exactly what's happening. Where's Tilly?'

'We were surfing, in front of the golf club. I couldn't find Tilly and then they turned off the lights . . .'

'You couldn't find Tilly?'

'She'd fallen in, or . . . I don't know. I don't *know* what happened. We just have to go.'

Ivan looked at me for one second, as if everything I just

116

said to him was rushing into his brain all at once. Then he turned and thumped twice on the side of the caravan.

'Dad!' he shouted. 'Dad!'

I covered my mouth and backed away, huddling against the canvas wall of the tent. I was shivering. My damp rashvest and boardies still clung to me, but I didn't *feel* anything. Dad came out and Ivan explained in short urgent rapidfire what had happened.

Dad grabbed his keys from inside the caravan door. 'I'm going up to the golf club to get them to turn the lights back on. Ivan, get everyone you can down on the beach. You'll need torches and blankets and as many first aid kits as you can get in case . . .' For the first time Dad looked at me. His face was like stone. Then his eyes snapped away again. 'Go now,' Dad said to Ivan.

I ran outside after Dad as he unlocked the car. 'I have to go too. Please.'

'Stay here,' Dad said, curtly. 'Get dressed.'

I grabbed his arm but he shook me off.

Dad climbed into the car. 'Stay here,' he barked. 'Jessica, get her inside.'

Mum was behind me. She wrapped her arms around me, more to restrain than comfort. Ivan had roused Tilly's family, and Ivan and Tilly's dad were going from tent to tent, caravan to caravan, while Tilly's mum and Teddy headed straight down to the beach with a torch. Tilly's Mum was holding Teddy close to her side. I watched other people emerge, carrying torches, blankets and first aid kits.

'I have to go,' I said to Mum. I was still shivering and my knees were weak. I tried to wriggle out of her grip, my legs buckling, but she held on with surprising strength.

'Come on, Zara,' she said. 'Come on, sweetie.' She was pulling me back into the annexe. Ivan and Tilly's dad walked past me. Neither of them looked at me. I realised I was making this weird high-pitched sound with my breathing. I scared myself with it, it wasn't me.

I kept begging. 'I have to help them look. I have to find her. Please. Don't make me stay here. Let me find her. Please let me find her.' But I collapsed against Mum. I was too weak to actually follow them. The words kept tumbling out, as if I was praying, 'Please, let me find her.' Over and over again.

Mum got me inside the caravan. She rubbed me down with a towel, pulling off my wet surf gear and making me put on trackies and a fleece and thick socks. She gave me two small white pills and I took them without even asking what they were. Within about twenty minutes I felt a hot glueiness spread through my body and I curled up on Mum and Dad's bed. I lay there watching Mum who was sitting at the kitchen table reading by lamplight, looking anxiously from time to time out the caravan door. I must have gone to sleep because when I stirred later she wasn't there. I tried to sit up, but I couldn't make my body work and I drifted off to sleep again.

When I finally woke, the day was bright outside. The caravan was empty. My head throbbed, my body ached. I lay there for a moment. They'd left me to sleep. Did that mean Tilly hadn't been found? Or did it mean she had?

I was gutless. I was too scared to go out at first. As long as I stayed in the caravan, already heating up in the morning sun, then I could believe anything I wanted. Finally I got up. I peeled off the clothes I'd slept in and pulled on underwear and a T-shirt and denim skirt that were laid out neatly by the bed.

The door to the annexe was zipped open and I squinted at the sunlight pouring in. Outside, Dad was crouching over some fishing gear.

'Tilly?' I asked. My mouth was dry and hardly any sound came out. I licked my lips. 'Tilly?' I asked again. 'Did you find her?'

Dad stood up. 'We found her.'

'Is she —?' I couldn't finish the question.

'She's at the hospital.'

'The hospital?' I repeated numbly.

'They want to keep an eye on her. She was developing hypothermia, they were worried about a head injury . . .'

'Head injury?'

'She was conscious, Zara. That's all I know. Ivan found her.'

I sat down on one of the camp chairs. Dad barely looked at me. He went back to untangling his fishing line.

'Dad?'

'Yes, Zara?'

'I'm sorry. I'm really sorry.'

'It's not me you need to apologise to.'

'I know.'

Dad shook his head, not even looking up. 'I just don't

understand you, Zara. You have everything. A beautiful home. A stable family. Everything you've ever asked for, we've bought you.'

I covered my face with my hands. Those pills Mum had given me had turned me to liquid. I was soupy and slow but everything else seemed harsh and bright.

'I scrape pretty girls up off the street every day. Just like you. They think they're indestructible. They think it won't be them in a car accident, or overdosing on drugs, or raped. It won't be them that gets into trouble. I don't get it. What makes them so special?'

Was he talking about Rio? But Rio *had* been okay in the end. I'd seen her a week after the accident, at the movies. She was fine. Scratched and bruised, but nothing that wouldn't heal.

Dad drove me home that night. The night of the party. One of the uniforms must have called him and he'd shown up in our car. He hadn't said anything, that night or since. The silence between us was shattering. It was the same silence, the things he *wasn't* saying, that I heard now. I knew he didn't mean Rio *or* Tilly. He meant me.

'I get it, Dad,' I said, flatly. 'I'm not special.'

'You're just like your mother,' Dad said, standing up with his fishing rod. 'You only hear what you want to hear. You twist everything I say.'

Is that why you stopped talking, I wanted to ask him? Is that why you stopped talking to her? To me? But he was gone before I'd even opened my mouth to speak.

Chapter Fourteen
Tilly

Usually I'd be kind of into being in hospital. You know, doctors and nurses fussing around, bringing jelly and icecream, people visiting with flowers and magazines, sneaking chocolate past the nurses. If it had just been my appendix or my tonsils it might have been kind of fun.

As it was I just felt lumpish and stupid, propped up on the hospital bed. I was sure the nurses thought I was a bit of a pest, that I'd brought it on myself and I was taking up a perfectly good hospital bed that could have been used by some poor old dying person or a lady having a baby. I felt guilty about how worried Mum and Dad and Teddy were last night, hovering over me. I squirmed with embarrassment when I remembered that someone – had it been

Ivan? I remembered he was there – had pulled off my wet clothes and wrapped me in blankets. I think Sawyer had been there too; I have this vague memory of him standing over the couch, frowning at me, while I was waiting for the ambulance. Why was he frowning? Was he still angry with me for pulling away from our kiss?

After the golf club lights went out, I'd heard Zara calling me. I tried to call back to her but I couldn't; my lips and face, even my larynx all felt numb. So I just kept swimming towards the sound of her voice. But then she must have decided to go in, because her voice wasn't there anymore, and there was nothing to swim towards. The darkness was complete and terrifying. There was no sound except the sloshing sea and my own rasping breath.

Can I tell you that I almost gave up then? I kind of did give up in a way. I turned onto my back and floated. I think – surely it's impossible – but I think I even slept, only for seconds at a time because the water would tug my legs down and I'd have to kick them back up to stay afloat. I was so cold. I couldn't remember if you could die of being cold, which is stupid because we did hypothermia last year in first aid. After a while, I thought I remembered that the moon had been in the opposite sky from the golf club, so I lay with my feet pointing at the moon, and keeping my eyes fixed on it, I kicked my legs.

Turned out I was right about the moon. The waves helped to carry me back to shore. When I hit sand, I thanked all the gods and goddesses profusely as I turned around and crawled up onto the beach. That's when I found Zara's board. I knew she'd left it like that so she could come back for me, so I collapsed underneath it, planning to catch my breath and then head up to the campsite.

But I couldn't catch my breath. There was ferocious stinging pain coming from my head. I reached up to touch it and — you know how you think these things at the weirdest times? — I remembered I'd cut my hair. I even felt kind of sad about it. I couldn't quite remember what I looked like, and if I couldn't remember maybe nobody could and maybe that meant that no one would find me.

I found a sticky spot on my head, and I was investigating it with my fingers when I realised it was blood. I think that was when I threw up. I rolled over onto my side. I don't know how long I lay there. I'd like to say I slept, but I didn't. I just kept torturing myself with these awful thoughts, that I would bleed to death, that children would find me on the beach in the morning, that the tide would take me and I'd be eaten by something.

Then the golf club lights came back on. I remember sitting up, trying to call out. Then I blacked out. It's crazy because this is the good bit, this is where Ivan found me and I was rescued, but I don't really remember it very well. I remember all the bad stuff, but I don't remember him discovering me, or carrying me in his arms, or laying me out on the couch. (I'm kind of glad I don't remember him undressing me, though.)

Mum came in with a cup of coffee. 'Hey, you're awake again. How are you feeling?'

'Okay.'

She sat down by the bed. 'Are you sure?'

'I'm fine.' I knew Mum wouldn't buy that. She's a psychotherapist, remember? Which is why I added quickly, 'Can we not talk about it?'

Mum burst into tears.

'Oh, Mum. Oh, don't *cry*. I'm sorry.' I floundered about looking for tissues but couldn't find any.

'I just . . .' Mum wiped her snot away with her hand. Classy woman, my mother. 'I was just so . . . I'm still so worried about you. What were you *doing* out there? Why would you take such an enormous risk? You could have been . . . you were nearly killed, Tilly. It's just not like you.'

'Well, sorry to be obvious, but, that's kind of the point. The not being like me bit.'

'But . . .' Mum shook her head. 'But you're such a fantastic kid. Why would you want to change?'

'I'm not a kid,' I moaned. 'Mum, it's great that you think I'm so swell. But you are my mother. You have to like me.'

'I don't *have* to do anything. I see plenty of people come into my practice who don't like their own children.'

'Am I in trouble?'

'Tilly, like you said, you're not a kid. You're nearly an adult. It doesn't work like that anymore. I mean, I don't even know how to punish you for something like that.'

'Are you angry?'

'I'm bloody furious! So's your dad. You can't imagine what it was like for us last night, what it was like for Teddy. I never want to go through anything like that again.'

'I'm never going to do anything like that again,' I promised.

'Trust is fragile, Tilly. Very fragile. It will take more than just promises. I think you'll find we're all a bit wary for a while.'

I looked up. Ivan was standing in the doorway. Had he heard the whole conversation? Mum was wrong, there were a million ways to punish me, and I was going to have to live them all.

He coughed. 'Ah, excuse me. I came to see if Tilly was feeling better.'

'I'm fine,' I said. I looked at Mum, pleadingly. 'I just want to get out of here.'

Mum stroked my cheek gently with her hand. It was reassuring; even if she was mad with me, I felt like her sick child again. 'They just want to keep you in for observation,' Mum said. 'You'll be more comfortable here than in a tent. You'll get more rest.'

'Except that they keep waking me up every hour!' I protested.

'To make sure you don't have permanent brain damage,' Mum pointed out. 'That's why they call it observation.'

'Yeah, yeah.'

'She's all yours,' Mum said to Ivan. 'She's a bit cranky.'

'Mum!'

'We're still going to talk about this,' Mum said to me. So that was my real punishment. Mum the psychotherapist.

When Mum had gone, Ivan sat down. 'How are you feeling?'

'I already said I'm fine.' I know, I know. Being grouchy meant I didn't have to thank him for saving my life.

'I can go if you . . .'

'No, no, don't go,' I said, 'I'm sorry.' I said it again to the world, 'I'm so freaking *sorry*, all right?'

Ivan perched awkwardly. He was regretting coming, I could tell.

'Is Zara okay?' I asked.

Ivan shrugged. 'She was still asleep when I left. I think Mum gave her something.'

'Oh.'

'Look,' Ivan said. 'I just came to apologise.'

'What for? Rescuing me?'

Ivan looked confused. 'I didn't rescue you,' he said. 'There was a group of us looking on the beach. Your dad carried you to the golf club.'

'Oh.' So Ivan hadn't carried me up to the golf club. That was kind of a let down. Though it was comforting, picturing Dad carrying me up the beach. Poor Dad.

Ivan pressed on. 'I wanted to apologise because you wouldn't have done this if it hadn't been for me. I was the one who told you to keep an eye on her. On Zara.'

'Oh, that.' I shook my head, dismissively. 'Seriously,

don't worry about it. I wanted to do it. I wasn't just following Zara. Hard as I'm sure it is to believe, that was me out there. That was Tilly.'

Ivan shook his head. Obviously he didn't believe me. 'I feel responsible.'

'Ugh,' I said. I couldn't cope with this anymore. My throbbing head injury was making me impatient. 'Ivan, you had nothing to do with it. Give me a bit more credit than that. You need to get over yourself.'

Ivan blinked. 'I didn't mean to imply . . .'

'That's the problem,' I snapped. 'Your whole family doesn't want to imply, suggest, state, infer . . . none of you *says* anything. If you're so worried about Zara, go find her and have an actual conversation. Talk to Zara yourself, instead of getting me to spy on her.'

Miriam, the duty nurse who'd introduced herself to me at breakfast, came in. Ivan was still blinking.

'I hope you're not upsetting my patient,' Miriam said, picking up my chart. She read through the notes. 'Now, Tilly, I need to ask if you've had a bowel movement this morning.'

Punish me for I have sinned. Ivan got up to leave.

'Don't leave on my account,' said Miriam.

'Thanks for coming,' I said weakly. 'You know, I probably shouldn't have . . .'

'You're welcome,' Ivan said stiffly. He didn't look back as he walked out the door. Moments later, Sawyer walked in. They would have passed each other in the corridor.

'How many boyfriends have you got, girl?' Miriam said.

'None,' I said. 'And my . . . *movements* are fine.'

'Uh huh.' She put a pill and a glass of water on my bedside table. 'This one will knock you out, so you might want to wait a little while before you take it. Not too long, now,' she said to Sawyer.

'Cripes, Tilly,' he said cheerfully. 'You look awful.'

'Thanks. My day's just getting better and better.'

'Sorry.' Sawyer pulled the chair closer to the bed and sat down on it. 'I brought you chocolate.'

'Thank you,' I muttered. 'Why are you here?'

'To see if you were alive,' Sawyer said. 'You know, Tilly, you're a difficult woman to please.'

I looked at him. His eyes were all twinkly. I think it was the head injury talking because I said, 'Why do you like me?'

'Because,' he shrugged. 'You're different from other girls.'

I grunted.

'You're kind of feisty and smart and timid and brave and stupid. You're a big mess of contradictions. Plus you've got great –'

'Yeah, shut up,' I warned.

'Hair.' He reached over and tugged tentatively at a bit of non-existent fringe that wasn't covered by bandage, then his fingers ran gently down my cheekbone. 'Why *don't* you like *me*?' Sawyer asked.

'Who says I don't like you?' I said, temporarily weakened by the cheekbone manoeuvre.

'Well, I know you do really.'

I hit his arm.

'But why did you run away last night? I thought we were having fun. I just wanted to get to know you.'

'Because it was a costume. It wasn't real. You only started liking me when I started dressing like . . . like Zara.'

'Are you kidding? I started liking you way before that, when you were at the golf club, trying not to laugh at your mate Zara being snooty and then you laughed anyway and it was this big, fantastic . . . and you were funny and sweet and daft. Besides, you weren't the only one in a costume last night. Do you think I wear a tux all the time? Do you think that's who *I* am?'

'I don't know who you are. I hardly know anything about you. And you don't know who I am.'

'That's the point,' Sawyer said. 'It's the finding out that makes this fun.'

'But what if we don't like each other?'

'Tilly, are you seriously going to miss out on this, on whatever might be happening between us, just because it might not work out?'

'I don't know. Maybe.' I turned to face the wall. I know. I'm such an idiot. Here was this great guy, sitting by my self-inflicted hospital bed while I looked like death warmed up, telling me he wanted to get to know me, telling me I looked bloody awful and that I was funny and that I have great hair. But I couldn't help it. I just didn't think I could put myself out there. Look at what had happened last night. Maybe some people weren't supposed to take risks. Maybe Mum was right, why was I trying to change myself? Wasn't I fine the way I was? Before Sawyer came along?

I looked at his mouth, and felt a shiver of the bliss I'd experienced the night before when he was kissing me. But just because it felt good, felt fantastic, felt perfect for a moment, didn't mean it was worth the heartache, the beating, the near-death experience that would inevitably follow if I lost my footing, if I fell.

Miriam poked her head in the door. 'You'd better take that pill now, girl.'

Sawyer pushed his chair back. 'All right, then,' he said, regretfully. 'See you, Tilly. It's been nice not getting to know you.'

And then Sawyer was gone. I took the pill. Miriam was right: I slept.

Chapter Fifteen
Zara

By lunchtime I could barely keep my eyes open. My neck ached, my body felt heavy and leaden, I couldn't hold myself up. I couldn't tell if it was tiredness or the after effects from the sedatives Mum had given me. But I lay down on Mum and Dad's bed and went to sleep. It was like crawling into a bag of cotton wool, the caravan was so hot and stuffy. I woke a couple of hours later to the sound of my mobile ringing, my throat dry, my head throbbing. I rolled over and squinted. The call screen was green – friends. I didn't want to talk to anyone, not even my friends. Behind my eyes I felt bruised, in fact I felt battered all over.

I sat up. No one was around outside. I went to the toilets and washed my face, drank water from the tap. I felt numb.

Maybe it was still Mum's drugs. Maybe it was just me. This numbness. This blankness. This failure to connect. With Tilly. With my mum, my dad. With Marcus.

'It's not just about sex,' Marcus had told me that night. 'I want to connect. I want to find a way in.' He tapped my chest. 'I want you to let me in *here*.'

He wanted to connect. Shouldn't I want that too?

And earlier that night Kayla had said to me as we downed our first vodka shots, 'He really loves you, Zara. Aren't you worried that you'll lose him?'

What was I waiting for? Wasn't everyone already doing it? Tang Yi was on the pill. Her sister had found the packet and all hell had broken loose. Her parents threatened to send her to live with some aunt in Shanghai. Tang Yi was scathing, 'They always say they want me to be a real Australian girl. They won't send me back to China.' She set her jaw. 'Anyway, I'd just run away. Go and live with Michael.' She was right, they didn't send her anywhere. But a few weeks later, Tang Yi said to me softly, as we waited in line at the cafeteria, 'My parents don't look me in the eyes anymore.' Was it worth it? Michael went to uni and studied engineering. He drove a car. She didn't talk about him much, but we all knew it was serious.

Rio talked about her sex life all the time, in way more detail than any of us wanted to hear. She talked about places she and Dante had done it, places they wanted to do it, what she did to him, what he did to her. 'If she's not careful,' Kayla said, 'she's going to get a reputation.'

Sooz wasn't doing it. She told me she wasn't ready. Was Kayla? I had never asked. (Don't ask, don't tell, remember?) I'm pretty sure she'd assumed Marcus and I were. But then Marcus had confided in Kayla. I don't know when or where, I never could figure that out. After that Kayla had seemed to take up Marcus's cause.

Why had Kayla been so desperate for me to have sex with Marcus when she was so willing to take my place? That night at the party, within half an hour of me breaking up with him, she was down on her knees, ready to . . . 'connect'. Were they already doing it, before that night? I knew the answer – of course they were. But how long for? Did he love her? Somehow, given the text message I'd received from him a few days ago, I doubted it.

I held my hair back in a ponytail and looked at my face in the mirror. There I was, this face, the smooth planes of my cheeks, blue eyes, eyebrows, lips. But what was under all that? What about me *mattered*? Dad was right. I wasn't special. I dropped my hair again.

As I walked back towards the caravan I could hear the phone ringing again. I spun on my heel and went down to the beach. The sky was overcast, the air was stiflingly humid.

There were people dotted all over the beach, couples and family groups, paddling in the shallows of the water, swimming, surfing, just hanging out together. I picked up my feet and started to jog towards the jagged rocks at the other end of the beach from where Dad went fishing. No one much ever went there. I didn't want to see anyone. I was especially dreading facing Tilly's parents and Teddy.

My head ached but I kept jogging, my feet landing with dull thuds on the sand. I saw the path to the Point Block headland and ran towards it, entering the bush where the steep zigzag path began. I wanted to push my body's boundaries, to feel my calves burning, to stretch my hamstrings. I wanted to be nothing but muscles and tendons and guts. I ran harder, stumbling on the uneven path. I fell forwards and caught myself, and my hands tore open on the gravelly path. I brushed off the dirt without stopping to inspect them, though I could feel a hot sting, and kept running.

We hadn't driven far from Kayla's house that night when I realised Lochie was drunk. But he wasn't just drunk – he was freaking insane. He got to the roundabout at the end of Kayla's street and drove round it three or four times, spinning his wheels. Rio squealed.

'Hey, careful,' Dante complained, but he didn't sound like he cared much. I could still hear the occasional moan from the back seat. I stared out the window.

When we got to the main road Lochie went through the red light. The tyres squealed as he turned the corner. He coasted onto the wrong side of the road then back again. Maybe he was just showing off. He obviously thought it was hilarious because he kept doing it. I ignored him. I just set my jaw and stared out my window and didn't say anything. I was bored. Even as the car swung back and forth between the lanes on the empty road, even as he ran red lights, even as the car spun out of control, as we finally veered off the road and hit a telegraph pole and the car folded in on itself with a sickening crunch of metal, I'd never been more bored in my life. I was rigid with it. I didn't care. I didn't care what happened to me, to Rio or Dante or Dante's brother. I thought about Marcus's face when I'd walked in on him and Kayla, and I didn't care about them either. On the outside I was Zara. Inside I was this big swirling nothing.

I was breathless as I neared the top of the path. My hands were bleeding, I could feel pieces of gravel embedded in them. My legs were burning from the run and my head pounded as my heart pumped blood. My mouth and throat were dust-dry but I hadn't thought to bring water with me.

From up here all the people playing at the water's edge looked busy but insignificant compared to the overwhelming blankness of the sea. It was like they were part of the white foam, but what was really important, what really meant something, was the vacant spreading grey-blue behind them, stretching out forever.

The funny thing was, Dad was right, but he was also totally wrong. I never actually believed that I was special. Underneath the face, the C cup, the golden-girl exterior, I'm pretty sure there's always been nothing. Nothing much at all.

I thought I'd found a safe hiding spot. But Ivan found me.

'What do *you* want?' I asked as he sat down. 'Did you follow me?'

'Zara, believe it or not my world doesn't revolve around you. I'm just walking.'

'Fine.'

Ivan sighed. 'I went to see Tilly this morning, in case you care. Apparently she's going to be fine.'

I didn't say anything. I kept staring at the smooth sea, where Tilly and I had surfed the night before. It was calm and still, there was nothing out there.

'Anyway, Tilly seems to think our whole family's kind of . . .' He faltered.

'Screwed?' I asked. Did Tilly think I was screwed too? Did she hate me?

'I was going to say emotionally dysfunctional.'

'Screwed,' I said.

'Yeah, well . . . screwed.' Ivan stared down at the beach. 'I love it up here,' he said, 'away from the crowds.' Then he said, 'Have you ever seen the Doves with each other? Have you watched how they talk to each other?'

'Yeah,' I said. I looked out at the sea. Blankness. But maybe there were some little white peaks way out there. Maybe something, far off, was building.

'How do *we* do that?' Ivan asked.

I looked at myself and then over at him. I'd pulled my feet up on the seat, my arms wrapped around my legs. Ivan's elbows rested on his knees and his hands were clasped in front of him. We were as far apart as we could be on a bench seat, each of us closed up so tightly. 'I don't know,' I said.

'Zara, what's going on with you this summer?' Ivan asked.

'Nothing's going on.'

'I know someone's been sending you text messages. You hold your phone like it's a loaded gun. Is someone giving you a hard time?'

Waves broke on the shore but then the sea sucked them back out again. It was like the waves were trying to escape, trying to break free, but how could they? The undertow owned them. They were just more sea, those waves, there was nowhere for them to go but under.

'No,' I said quietly. 'It's no one.'

'What about that guy you were seeing, Marcus? He doesn't come around anymore. Did you break up? Is he hassling you?'

I shrugged.

'Come on, Zara. At least I'm trying!'

'I never *asked* you to. I came up here to be alone.'

'Alone like Mum? Alone like Dad? Because I don't want to be like that.' His voice cracked. 'And I don't think you do either. Tilly's right, Zars. Our family's broken. It's toxic. I don't want to be like *them*.' I was shocked to see a tear sliding down his cheek. He rubbed it angrily away with the ball of his palm.

'Neither do I,' I said, relenting. But my eyes were dry. My whole skin was dry, like someone had sucked all the moisture out of me.

We sat like that together. We didn't say anything. But

you know . . . it kind of didn't suck to have him there. After a while, the wind seemed to change direction, to spring right off the sea. There was a chill in the air that made me shiver. Without saying anything both of us got up as the cool change drifted in and we walked side by side, back down to the emptying beach.

Chapter Sixteen
Tilly

Although I'd spent the whole day complaining about being in the hospital, when Dr Liew came to see me at breakfast the next morning and declared me fit to return to the campsite, I suddenly wanted to bury my head under my pillow and stay.

That is, until Dr Liew said, 'But before you go, I'd like you to have a quick chat to one of our resident counsellors.'

I sat up. 'Do I have to? My mum's a psychotherapist. Couldn't I just talk to her?'

The doctor smiled apologetically. 'Your mum suggested the counsellor. But I think you'll like Jo.'

She wasn't what I'd been expecting. I might have liked her if we'd met at uni or something. She was youngish, and kind of, well, out there, with a big blue streak in her hair, thick-rimmed black glasses and really dark lipstick.

Jo asked to see my arms. That was weird. Was she a head doctor or an arm doctor? It was only as she was running her fingers lightly over my pale flabby arms that I realised she was checking to see if I was injecting myself with drugs.

'Please!' I said, giggling because her finger tickled my inner elbow. 'As if. I am the most boring person in the world.'

'Well, people don't usually do drugs because they find themselves wildly fascinating,' Jo pointed out.

'What about rockstars? And supermodels?'

Jo made a noise that sounded like *pishaw*. 'Spoilt rotten, the lot of them.'

'That's your professional opinion?'

Jo tilted her head and looked at me as if she was thinking about it. 'Well, okay. If you want an honest answer, I think it's an industry that's very big on surfaces. These people are being constantly judged, assessed, objectified, based on outward appearances. Even talented musicians or actors, especially women, are constantly being held up to un-achievable, unhealthy standards in terms of body image. Perhaps there's a disconnect between mind and body that they seek to rectify artificially through drugs. But I still think that being spoilt is part of it. Many of them are used to having things come easily. Drugs are a quick short-term solution and only serve to compound the long-term problem.' Jo pointed at two chairs by the window. I got off the bed. It made me feel better to be sitting at her level.

'Well, my mind and body are fine. No drugs for me.'

'Sometimes, in my work, I find that intelligent people have a similar disconnect, but it's the body, the exterior, that's missing in the equation rather than the mind.'

'Huh. Is that so?'

'Tilly, do you have a boyfriend?'

'Did my mum ask you to ask me that?'

'No, of course not. You know this is confidential.'

I shrugged. 'Well, I don't anyway.'

'Are you sexually active?'

'Uh . . . *no*.'

Jo had a habit of pausing after each answer, as if she was giving me time to elaborate. Mum did the same thing. So I sat there and said nothing. But I knew silence could be interpreted too.

'How do you feel about that?' Jo asked finally.

'Dandy. Can we talk about something else?'

'Sure. What would *you* like to talk about?'

'Well. I guess you want to know why I went surfing at night.'

'Sure,' Jo said again. 'Tell me about it.'

'I don't know why. I just did. But I wasn't trying to . . . you know. Top myself or anything.'

'Okay. Have you ever thought about topping yourself?'

'No way.'

'Okay.'

141

'Aren't you going to write this stuff down in a notebook?'

'Would you like me to write it down?'

'I'm just thinking about saving you a bit of work later on,' I said sniffily.

'Have you talked to your parents about what happened?' Jo asked.

'Some. I know I'll have to talk about it a lot. Mum will want to psychoanalyse my guts out. The surfboard, the foaming waves. It's all totally Freudian.'

Jo smiled. 'Do you get on with your mum?'

I leaned forward with my hands clasped and said, 'So . . . vot do you zink about your mother?'

Jo leaned back in her chair. 'Look, Tilly, here's the lowdown. I don't get the sense that you're a danger to yourself or others, nor that you're particularly disturbed, so I'm fine with you going home today.'

'Pleased to hear it,' I muttered ungratefully (but secretly I *was* quite pleased to hear it).

'But I do think you have some unresolved issues,' Jo went on. 'You're edgy when I ask you about boyfriends or sex, and you keep bringing Freud up – clearly there's something going on that you're not telling me. I think you're deflecting my questions so you don't have to face these issues. What worries me is that you participated in uncharacteristic and extremely risky behaviour, resulting in what could be considered a serious accident.' She looked at me seriously. 'You could have died, Tilly.'

I stared down at my hands. 'I don't want to die,' I said.

I looked at her and this time I made myself hold her gaze. 'I really don't.'

'I believe you. But you need to face things head on.'

'Like that's easy.'

'You don't have to do it alone. It's up to you, Tilly. We can end the session now if you want.' Jo sat poised, looking at me.

'I really don't know why I did the night surfing,' I said.

'Do you want to find out?'

'What you said before, about bodies and brains . . . I used to wonder, why do we even have bodies? I mean, our minds do all the important things—think, dream, imagine, create. Our bodies, well, they just seem to be all about sustaining our minds. You know, we eat and procreate and defecate . . . it's all about keeping the body healthy so we can make more bodies. It seems so inefficient.'

'Is that really what you think your body is for?'

I thought about Sawyer, about the ecstasy I'd felt for that fleeting moment last night when I'd finally caught a wave. 'I guess not.'

'Our bodies let us communicate, experience touch, sight, sound, smell, taste. Our bodies let us interact with our environment. Our bodies sing and dance and play the piano, kiss, wave goodbye, cry, laugh.'

'But how do we trust what our bodies tell us? All these sensations, these conflicting feelings . . . How do we know the right thing to do?'

'What do you think?' Jo asked me.

'We use our judgement,' I said. 'We learn from past experience. We use our imagination. It still comes back to our brain.'

'Some people would say the brain is the erotic centre of the body.'

'Eew.'

'Do you think of your body as your friend?' Jo asked me.

'I hate questions like that.'

'Fair enough.'

'You know, all that *do you love yourself?* stuff. I mean, if you say you do love yourself, then you're arrogant or vain. If you say you don't then you have self-esteem issues.'

'Do you think you have self-esteem issues?'

I shrugged. 'Doesn't everyone?'

'Not everyone goes surfing in the dark and nearly dies,' Jo pointed out.

'I wasn't the only one, you know,' I said.

'I know. But you're here. If your friend wants to talk to me she'd be welcome too.'

I looked out the window. It wasn't a great view, I could see into the concrete carpark, could see the other brown stained hospital buildings. I looked at the tips of my fingers resting on the arm of the chair, then down at my body. I thought again about kissing Sawyer, how far I had wanted things to go with him, and how far away I'd pulled. Were some risks worth taking? Had I stuffed everything up?

'You know how I said I don't have a boyfriend,' I said. 'Well. There is this one guy . . .'

Chapter Seventeen
Zara

I was standing by the gate waiting for Tilly when they arrived. The cool change hadn't stuck; the next morning the sun was hotter than ever. I didn't know what time Tilly was due back, but in the end I'd gotten tired of hanging around the caravan with Mum hovering nervously over me, so I headed up to the roadside to wait. I felt bad that I hadn't been to see Tilly at the hospital but I was also scared of facing her — facing her whole family. Did Tilly hate me? Did all the Doves hate me? That lovely family, was I public enemy number one? I just wanted to see her now, to get seeing her over and done with.

But it wasn't Tilly I saw. Of course they caught my eye, two full-on city girls walking up an otherwise deserted road in the middle of nowhere. I recognised Kayla first, her distinctive blonde-streaked hair that sits up in elastic coils all over her head.

It was *surreal* to see them walking towards me. They didn't belong here. They were plastic, bright and shiny but totally fake, compared to the dusty gums, the brown road. Sooz tall like me, Kayla ever so petite, like a doll.

But it was all part of The Plan. That stupid plan which had been born at the mall after school one day near the end of term.

'So anyway,' Kayla had said as she adjusted a skirt over her hips. 'I told my parents, how can you buy a holiday house without even asking me. Don't you care about me at all? I mean, where's Alder Springs anyway? No one's ever even heard of it, am I right?' Then she turned to us. 'Does this make me look fat?' She turned back to the mirror. 'I said, I hope it's got a sauna and a pool. They think it will be a good chance to spend more time together. What's with that? Like we don't see enough of each other! We all live in the same house.'

Sooz made commiserating noises.

'I know where Alder Springs is,' I said, flicking through the belts hanging up outside the changeroom. 'It's about thirty minutes inland from Indigo.'

The Plan, mostly devised so that Kayla didn't have to spend more time with her parents, was that Sooz would go to Alder Springs with Kayla and they'd both come and visit me in Indigo; and then another day, Dad would drive me to Alder Springs to hang out with them. I'd terminated The Plan in my head the second I walked in on Marcus and Kayla. Only I realised now that I'd never actually texted Sooz to call it off.

Sooz saw me first. 'Zara!' She swiped me on the arm. 'Don't you answer your phone anymore?'

'Hi.' I said.

Kayla sashayed up and air-kissed my cheeks. She looked around. 'Oh my godfather, is this, like, the total wilderness or what?'

'Well, it is camping,' I said, edgily. 'It's not supposed to be a five-star resort.'

'Kayla's parents dropped us off in Indigo this morning. We're going to meet them at the golf club for dinner. You're invited too, of course.'

'Great.' What if I didn't want to be invited?

Sooz looked a bit hurt. 'You did remember we were coming?'

I shrugged. What could I do? They were here now. I started walking down the gravel road, back into the campground and Sooz loped along beside me. Kayla tottered after us.

'So what is there to do in this place?' Kayla asked, placing her strappy sandals preciously on the ground, one foot after another, as though she was scared dirt was permanent. She looked around distastefully at the bush. 'The town was,' like, totally one-horse. Apart from the beach, that is, and you know I don't do sand.' Kayla was the kind of girl who thought everything about her was cute. Like, she thought it was cute that she didn't like going to the beach. Being helpless was cute. Having a thing about her shoes was cute. Having sex with my boyfriend behind my back, that was probably cute too.

'You're going to get pretty bored, then,' I said. 'This place is pretty much all about the beach.'

'Isn't there a pool or something?' Sooz asked tactfully.

'This isn't a resort. It's a foreshore campground.' I turned to Kayla and said, in a slightly challenging tone, 'Come on, Kayla. There's a big, beautiful ocean right there. We've even got a spare surfboard.' Though actually, we didn't. Ivan's was still lost. I wasn't going to tell them that, or how we'd lost it.

Kayla was about to say something, her eyebrows arching, when Tilly's car approached. We all stepped back off the road. Tilly was riding shotgun, her dad was driving. He pulled over and Tilly's window slid open.

'Hi, Zara,' Julian Dove called, as if everything was normal.

'Hi.' I leaned into the car. 'Hey, Tilly,' I said, self-consciously.

'Hey.'

'How are you feeling?'

Tilly pulled a face. 'I wish people would stop asking me that.' She glanced briefly at Sooz and Kayla then back at me. 'I'm fine,' she said, quietly.

I wanted to say how sorry I was. But I couldn't with

Sooz and Kayla standing right behind me. I stood back. 'See you down there?'

'Want a lift?' Julian asked.

I shook my head. 'We'll walk.'

'All right. See you on the flip side,' Julian said. The car continued to crunch along the gravel driveway.

'Who was *that*?' Kayla asked. I thought I could hear a sneering tone of judgement in her voice and for a moment I pictured Tilly how Kayla would have seen her, a little overweight, her pointy features, her plain clothes, no make-up.

'Just a friend,' I said.

'What was with her face?'

'What about her face?' I snapped.

'Her eyes looked all bruised.'

'Oh, that. She had an accident. She's been in hospital.'

'Oh. How freaky.'

'Yeah,' I said. 'Like, totally.' I kept my voice even and measured; I doubt Kayla realised I was making fun of her. But I was treading a thin line. Did I really want to do this? What was I trying to do, pick a fight? After all, I'd finished with Marcus. What did it matter if they were together?

'Shall we go back into town?' Sooz asked, eyeing me warily. She sensed the tension even if Kayla was oblivious. 'There was a semi-decent looking cafe. I'm sure we could get lattes.'

'That was miles back,' Kayla complained.

'It would be faster if we walked along the beach,' I said. I looked at Kayla. 'That is, unless you'd rather go by the road,' I offered.

'No, it's fine,' Kayla said, pouting slightly.

As we passed through the campground I looked longingly at Tilly's tent. She was sitting on a camping chair alone, though I could see her mum darting around. Tilly flipped up her hand in a wave and I waved back. I hadn't realised how much I'd missed her company until just then. Having Kayla and Sooz with me was so wrong it gave me a pain in my gut. As we walked on towards the beach, I wondered if Tilly was watching us.

Part of me wanted to turn to Kayla and Sooz and say, 'Sorry, I can't hang out with you today,' but I couldn't. They'd come all this way, it was only one day. Tilly would understand. And in the end, Tilly would be going back to her school and I'd have to deal with Sooz and Kayla for the rest of the year.

Still, I felt pretty crappy leaving Tilly behind.

At the top of the beach path, Kayla turned to me and said, suddenly, 'Haven't you got your phone on you? We tried to ring you, before.'

'Um, no.' I couldn't read her expression.

'We'll wait while you go back and get it,' Kayla said. She looked at her nails and frowned at a chip in her polish. Then she looked up at me and met my eyes. Her gaze was steady, wide-eyed. 'I gave my parents your number, my phone's low on batteries.'

I hesitated, looking from Kayla to Sooz. Sooz blinked, waving a stray fly away from her face.

'They might need to call us if they're running late or something,' Kayla pointed out.

'We don't mind waiting,' Sooz said.

I shrugged. 'Okay, I'll just get it.'

I turned and jogged back towards the caravan. I grabbed my phone and switched it on to check the power levels. Mum had charged it up again.

As I walked back towards Kayla and Sooz the phone chimed four times to let me know I had text messages. I stopped. I didn't want to look at them in front of Kayla and Sooz. Three of the messages were from them anyway. The last one was from *him*, from Number Withheld, sent yesterday afternoon. It said: *daddys got a gun*.

Ugh, that was creepy. What did that even mean? Was Number Withheld calling himself Daddy? Or was it about *my* father?

Maybe it was Lochie sending the messages. He knew Dad was a cop. He'd spat in my hair that night, when my dad came to pick me up. I was sitting on the kerb, feet in the gutter, arms around myself to stop myself from shivering; I'd left my long-sleeve in Kayla's room. Dad showed up in his uniform. I looked up and there he was, standing over me. I felt relieved, ashamed. I stood up and he steered me towards our car. Lochie had lobbed a gob of spit into my hair.

'You skanky cow!' he said. 'You fu–!'

One of the uniform cops had Lochie up against the car in a second.

Dad didn't look back. 'Don't you ever come near my daughter again,' he said. He didn't say it loudly, but his voice carried across the broken car, across the street, out over the city.

In the car Dad handed me a tissue. He said nothing. My stomach flipped as I remembered wiping the slimy, thick saliva out of my hair.

I shook the memory off. Anyway, Lochie didn't even know me. Why would he do this? But the point was it *could* be Lochie. It could be anyone. That was the real power of Number Withheld: this photo album of faces that flicked through my mind every time a number dropped into my inbox. Everyone I knew at school or work, people I'd met at clubs or parties, brothers of people I'd met at parties. People I didn't even remember meeting. Everyone was a suspect. That's what made me vulnerable.

As I walked back towards Kayla and Sooz, I saw Ivan coming towards me.

'You okay?' he asked.

After yesterday I kind of wanted to tell him about the message but Sooz and Kayla were waiting for me.

'I'm fine,' I said, glancing over at them.

'I see your friends are here.'

I nodded. I knew he thought my friends were shallow. Did he think I was too?

'Tilly's back from the hospital,' I told him.

'Oh. Good. Good.' He didn't exactly gush, but I could tell he didn't think Tilly was shallow.

I got back to the beach path, where Kayla and Sooz were waiting for me.

Over lattes Kayla and Sooz talked about some club they'd both been to in Melbourne, gushed over the cute guy in Alder Springs who gave Kayla a massage, and bitched about Ashley, who was going out with Kayla's ex-boyfriend. I stared out the window. I didn't care about Ashley. She was all right. Anyway, Kayla had broken up with Danny in Year 9 before boyfriends even counted. I guess it was all just regular gossip, but for some reason it bored me even more than usual. I missed Tilly.

Kayla got up to go to the toilet. Sooz and I looked at each other.

'So what have you been doing all summer?'

I knew Sooz wouldn't understand the night surfing. None of them would. They'd think it was weird. Dangerous and stupid. They'd think it was like that time one of the emo girls at school got caught in the toilets carving 'no life' into her arm with a razor and got suspended for bringing a weapon to school. Why doesn't anyone know what to do with unhappy people?

My phone chimed. I'd received another text message. Sooz looked at me expectantly. I looked down at the table.

'Aren't you going to check that?' Sooz asked me.

'No.'

'Wow. I just don't have that kind of willpower. I have

to check text messages the second they arrive.' Sooz tilted her head and studied me. 'Is something going on with you, Zara?'

'No.'

'You just . . . well, you haven't been yourself. We've all noticed. We've hardly seen you since school finished. You're screening calls, not answering your messages.'

Kayla came back. She looked from me to Sooz.

'It's nothing,' I said to Sooz.

'What's nothing?' Kayla asked.

'Zara just got a text message.'

'Who from?' Kayla asked.

'I don't know,' I told her.

'You don't know? Oh, that's so *weird*,' Kayla said, her face twisting with sympathy.

Sooz laughed. 'It's not *that* weird. Zara just didn't check it yet. See, Zara, normal people read their messages.'

I looked at Kayla. Our eyes met briefly and she looked away.

And that was when I knew it was Kayla. I knew that if I checked my phone the new message would be from Number Withheld, sent while she was in the toilets. I knew that if I demanded to see her phone, I'd be able to prove that she'd lied, that her batteries were just fine. A flood of euphoric relief swept through me. I was right. All the power of Number Withheld had been in the withholding of identity. Now I knew it was Kayla, the messages themselves meant nothing. They couldn't hurt me.

I kept looking at her, I refused to look away. She was caught out, and she knew it. The colour had drained from her face as she read and reread the blackboard of specials on the wall. But why? What had I ever done to her? She glanced back at me and this time she held my gaze. I saw a mix of emotions on her face. She looked ashamed, embarrassed to be caught out. But I also saw a set in her jaw — she was angry with me. But the loathing in her eyes wasn't just for me. It was herself she hated. It was probably Marcus too, mixed up with love, or whatever it was she'd felt for him as she'd given him what he wanted. I thought about the message I'd received from him the other day. Kayla had probably gone all the way with him, but he didn't want Kayla. Her eyes slid away again. I glanced down at the table. A smile tugged the corners of my mouth.

After that, the day was different. I was different. The tables had turned and I found I could be gracious, even friendly. Kayla's face was dark as she lagged slightly behind us walking through the town towards the golf club. Sooz prattled, encouraged by my newfound good humour, oblivious to the altered mood between Kayla and me.

Chapter Eighteen
Tilly

That night Mum and Dad decided to take me out for dinner, to the golf club. I went along, half hoping I'd see Sawyer, half hoping I wouldn't. It hadn't been a bad day in the end. Ivan had sat with me most of the morning and into the afternoon. He seemed to loosen up a bit around me and my dad. I mean, he was still retentive and everything. But we did the crossword together, the three of us, and Ivan even cracked a few jokes.

'Are you, like, being funny?' I asked him. 'Because I've got medication for that. I've got medication for everything.'

'I wouldn't stand for that if I were you,' Dad said to Ivan.

'It's all right, Professor Dove. I think Tilly's just talking to herself again. Maybe it's time for her pill.'

See what I mean?

'There's Zarsparilla,' Teddy said, pointing across the restaurant.

Zara was there with her friends, Sooz and Kayla. Shoes and Paler, Ivan called them. One of the girls' parents was with them too, they were all sipping champagne, even the girls. Zara caught my eye and waved. I waved back, but I got the distinct impression that now her real friends were here she didn't want me around.

Then Mum nudged me. 'There's your friend.'

'Zara?'

'No. Your *other* friend.'

Sawyer was waiting on Zara's table. 'Oh. Well, I don't know if he is still my friend.' I could see Paler simpering up at him. He turned and caught me looking at him. I wanted to hide. I knew everything I was feeling was probably written all over my face in fluorescent ink, but I refused to let myself look away. He winked. I winked back. He stopped and did a little theatrical double take. He looked over one shoulder and then the other and then pointed to himself with this quizzical expression. I just grinned, then crossed my eyes.

I turned to Mum. 'We're still friends,' I said. I felt like I might burst.

'Kissing friends?' Teddy asked.

'Excuse me!' I said. 'When I was your age I didn't know anything about kissing. I didn't even know kissing existed.'

'You did so,' Teddy said.

'Tilly?'

I looked up. It was Zara.

'We're going to hang out on the couches for a while,' she said. 'Want to join us?'

I looked at Mum. She nodded. 'Go on.'

'Doesn't your family hate me?' Zara asked as we walked towards her friends.

'No,' I said, surprised. 'I don't think so.'

'Tilly, I'm sorry.'

'It's fine,' I said. Fine was such a nothing word. But I didn't feel like I could really talk with Sooz and Kayla sitting right there, waiting for us.

Zara stopped, grabbing my arm so I stopped too. She looked deep into my eyes, and said, seriously, 'Tilly, I mean it. I'm so sorry. I'm sorry for taking you with me. I'm sorry for leaving you behind. For not visiting at the hospital. I almost got you killed.'

In a small voice I said, 'I don't want you to be sorry for taking me. I'm sorry I ruined it.'

'No, you didn't.'

I didn't answer, I looked away, blinking back threatening tears.

'You *didn't*, Tilly. It was too dangerous.'

'Not for you,' I protested.

'For me too. It could just as easily have been me as you.' We both had tears in our eyes now.

Her friend, Sooz, called out, 'You two look very serious.'

'Sorry,' Zara said. We went over and sat down on the couches with them.

'I love your hair,' Sooz said, genuinely.

I smiled, a little thinly. Actually, I loved it too now. It felt right for me, even if it was dramatic. Maybe I liked the drama. But I was sort of sick of talking about it.

'Thanks,' I said. 'It was Zara's idea.'

I was getting a vague glimmer of what it must be like to be Zara. The amount of people who commented on my hair, it was as if it was the most immediate, most important thing about me. They saw the haircut and thought that was who I was. For Zara, more so, because it was more than just a haircut, they were looking at a whole package – hair, face, body, clothes. She was like those rockstars: all people saw was the outside, this impossible-to-maintain perfection, as if nothing else about her mattered.

'Ooh, check him out,' Kayla said with cat-like vowels, not acknowledging me at all. Her eyes were following Sawyer around the room. 'He's so *hot*.'

'You're out of luck,' Zara said. 'He's only got eyes for Tilly.'

I tried to blush modestly. I'm sure I failed.

'Seriously?' Kayla said, with her eyebrows raised disbelievingly. Could she be more of a cow? 'But you're not, like, actually an item?'

'Actually,' Zara said, 'haven't you already got a boyfriend? As in my boyfriend? Not that we're *actually* an item anymore.'

Kayla looked paler (ha ha). Sooz looked uncomfortable. I guess she knew what Zara was talking about, even if I didn't.

'Hey, look, don't worry about it, Kayla,' Zara said. 'You're welcome to each other. But there is one thing.'

'What?' Kayla asked, sulkily.

'Well, do you think I should check that text message now? Or should I delete it?'

'I don't know.'

''Cause, see, I was thinking it might be evidence. I mean my dad's a cop. Tilly's dad is a law professor. I was sort of thinking that one of them might know about SMS and stalking laws. I'm pretty sure it's illegal.'

'Stalking?' Sooz said. She looked at Kayla then back to Zara. Then she looked at me, questioningly.

I still had no idea what Zara was talking about, but I chimed in. 'Oh, you should definitely keep it. It's evidence.'

'Well, whoever sent it withheld the number to conceal their identity,' Zara said, looking at me. Kayla looked like she wanted to crawl into the crack between the couch cushions.

'Oh, they can totally trace it,' I said, though I had no idea if it was true or not. But I added for good measure, 'Ask my dad. He wrote the course about technology and the law.'

Zara nodded. 'I'll do that.'

'You could join us for dinner now, if you want,' I offered. 'I mean, if you wanted to ask him about it.'

'Yeah, thanks,' Zara said. 'I think I do. Kayla, you'll explain to your parents, won't you? Sooz, see you later. I guess you'll get Kayla's side of the story, whatever that ends up being.'

'It's not my fault you can't take a joke,' Kayla said.

Zara turned her back on Kayla and Sooz. We walked over towards our table.

'Well,' said Zara, smiling weakly. 'I think I just lost all my friends.'

'Are you sure you want to come and sit with us? You could go back and . . .'

'Are you kidding?'

'Why didn't you tell me you were getting text messages?'

Zara shrugged. 'I don't know. I'm not used to . . . talking about stuff.' She rolled her eyes and said, 'It's the "don't ask, don't tell" policy.'

'I don't know what that is.'

'It's this thing of my mum's, about not telling people your secrets. You know, in case they use them against you. It's probably kind of stupid.'

'It sounds *lonely*, Zara.' For the first time, I actually felt sorry for Zara's mum. Did she still live by that rule? My mum and dad were best friends. They told each other everything. Keeping all your secrets sealed up inside you . . . it sounded seriously painful to me. I mean, I know I'm a total blabbermouth. I'll never be a mystery wrapped in an enigma. I'll never be Zara. But who wants to be? Not even Zara wanted to be Zara, as far as I could tell.

'Zara, there is one more thing.'

'Yeah?'

'My dad teaches politics. Not law.'

'Oh. Do we have to tell Kayla that?'

I nudged her. 'Your secret's safe with me.'

We got back to our table. Zara looked kind of shy, she hung back.

'Can Zara eat with us?' I asked.

'Yay!' Teddy said. Dad shifted his chair around to make room, then pulled an empty chair over from a neighbouring table.

'I need to tell the waiter to serve my food over here,' Zara said, though she sat down.

'The waiter, you say?' Mum asked. 'Hmm.'

They were all looking at me.

'All right,' I said. 'I get the hint.' I pushed my chair back and stood up. Sawyer was standing at the till writing up someone's bill. I waited for him.

'Hi,' he said, when he was finished.

'Hi.'

'Can I help you?'

'I have a message for you,' I said. I was trying to forget all the other people in the restaurant, watching me.

He stepped closer to me. His face was right there, above mine. Everyone else in the room instantly vanished.

'Yes?' he asked.

'Um, Zara's going to eat at our table.'

'The girl's actually got some taste.'

'So you need to, um, change the order.'

'Okay.' He was staring right into my eyes. 'It'll cost you,' he said.

'Oh yeah, we'll pay for her food.'

'Not that! I mean it will cost *you*.'

'Oh. *Oh.* You mean kissing, don't you?'

'Yes.' He laughed. 'I mean kissing.'

'My parents are right there.'

'So? *I'm* at work.'

'I never kissed a boy before. I mean, before you.'

'Really?' Sawyer said, uncaringly as I leaned towards him.

In the interests of being totally honest, I said, 'Well, there was this one time . . .'

'Tilly, shut up.'

It was short. (He *was* at work, and my parents *were* right there.) But it was extremely sweet.

Chapter Nineteen
Zara

After dinner, Tilly's parents left with Teddy. I waited by the restaurant windows as Tilly said goodbye to Sawyer so we could walk back together. Sooz came over to say goodbye, while Kayla waited at the door, her face stony.

I looked out at the surf, lit up by the club floodlights. The sun had just set and the sky was a totally mellow shade of navy blue fading to a pale line at the horizon. A few stars already glinted. I could feel an ache inside me. I wanted to be there, under that night sky. I felt guilty for wanting it after everything that had happened, but I couldn't make the feeling go away.

'Hey, Zara.'

I turned around. It was Chris, the guy who'd taught Mieke, Tilly and me to surf, those long summers ago. It seemed a distant time now, but having Chris standing next to me brought it back in a rush, the innocence of the waves.

'How's my star pupil?' he asked.

'Okay.' And I knew I would be. Okay, that is. But I kept my eyes on that dark-reaching ocean.

'Hear you've been doing a bit of soul-surfing.' I looked at him. He flashed a sheepish grin. 'That's what I call it. Out there at night, under the stars. Best time to surf, doing it by heart, using your gut. No crowds, no one dropping in . . . just pure stoke.'

'But isn't it too dangerous?' I asked.

Chris didn't even look at me as he answered with certainty. He was looking into that same ocean. What did he see? 'It's totally dangerous. There's consequences. But you know that. That's why we do it, right?'

Maybe some risks − *calculated* risks − were okay, were worth taking. Some weren't, for sure. Like getting in the car with Lochie, that was stupid. Not only that, it wasn't me, or who I wanted Zara Sutherland to be. I didn't want to be in the passenger seat. I wanted to be behind the wheel. But maybe it was okay, sometimes, to test the limits of yourself, to push your boundaries. After all, when you were right there, out in it, skimming the edge of the sky, that was when you knew you were alive. That was when *I* knew life was worth living.

Tilly came up and pushed an arm through mine. 'Ready?' she said.

I looked up, smiling goodbye. But Chris had gone.

'Ready,' I said. And together we walked out into the salty night air.

Chapter Twenty

Tilly

Zara and I were hanging out at my tent. She was painting her toenails, looking up every now and then with a smile on her face as she teased me about Sawyer. She was the most relaxed I'd seen her all summer.

We're nothing alike, Zara and I. She's tall and blonde and a total goddess, with little gold freckles that dance across her nose. She looks like she's been dipped in warm paint. I'm middle-sized and alternately round and pointy, I used to think in all the wrong places. But what do I know? My face was still sore, but I was beginning to look less like I'd lost a battle and more like someone who'd had a tumble and lived to tell the tale.

We weren't going anywhere that day, no plans. Just

mucking around, waiting to see what the day would bring us. Zara was laughing about something I'd said, and she circled her brush in the air, threatening to dot my nose with nail polish.

I looked up and there she was, walking up the path towards us. I think I mentioned she was short. But for a tiny person, she fills up a huge amount of space. She was wearing wide-legged Thai fisherman pants and a black crossover top. Her dark hair was in two plaits hanging either side of her head. She looked sweet, but also like she might be about to kick someone's ass, kung-fu style. She shielded her eyes, squinting into the sun, and smiled.

'Mieke!' I shouted.

Zara's head whipped around. She jumped up. 'Mieke! Mieke! Mieke!' she cried. She ran over with her arms out and so did I. Mieke looked a bit scared as we descended on her — we were weapons of mass affection. But Zara and I held on, dancing around in a circle and she danced too. When we finally let go, she stepped back a bit.

'So,' she said, 'did you miss me?'

About the author

Penni Russon grew up in Tasmania, roaming around on a small mountain and making up stories about imaginary lost pets with her best friend. She used to write poetry until she discovered novels were a lot more forgiving. The Undine trilogy, *Undine*, *Breathe* and *Drift*, published by Random House in Australia and Greenwillow in the US, is a series of books about a magical girl, set in Hobart's streets and the surrounding bush and seascapes. Penni lives in St Andrews, Victoria, with her husband and two daughters, and maintains a sometimes daily blog called Eglantine's Cake.

Find out more about Penni at:
eglantinescake.blogspot.com
www.pennirusson.com

MORE ♥ TITLES

TN/T

Please return / renew by date shown.
You can renew it at:
norlink.norfolk.gov.uk
or by telephone: 0344 800 8006
Please have your library card & PIN ready

5/12		

NORFOLK LIBRARY
AND INFORMATION SERVICE

penguin.co.uk/vintage